Yesterday's *Promise*

a novel

Vanessa Miller

WHITAKER
HOUSE

YESTERDAY'S PROMISE
Book One in the Second Chance at Love Series

Vanessa Miller
www.vanessamiller.com

ISBN: 978-1-60374-207-8
Printed in the United States of America
© 2010 by Vanessa Miller

Whitaker House
1030 Hunt Valley Circle
New Kensington, PA 15068
www.whitakerhouse.com

Library of Congress Cataloging-in-Publication Data

Miller, Vanessa.
  Yesterday's promise / by Vanessa Miller.
      p. cm. — (Second chance at love ; bk. 1)
  Summary: "When Melinda Johnson's father, the bishop of Omega Christian Church, goes back on his word and appoints her ex-fiancé, Steven Marks, as his successor instead of her, Melinda must decide whether to pursue her call to preach elsewhere or to stay at Omega and rekindle a relationship with Steven—even though he opposes female pastors"—Provided by publisher.
  ISBN 978-1-60374-207-8 (trade pbk.)
  1. African American churches—Fiction. I. Title.
  PS3613.I5623Y47 2010
  813'.6—dc22
                        2009042889

2 3 4 5 6 7 8 9 10 **LU** 16 15 14 13 12 11 10

Yesterday's Promise is romance at its best—warm, sweet, and brimming over with real people trying to follow God's Word, despite what others believe. Readers will delight in this tender story by Vanessa Miller.

—Jacquelin Thomas
Author, *Jezebel* and *The Ideal Wife*

The characters in *Yesterday's Promise* challenged my faith. They reminded me that God's promises are true yesterday, today, and forevermore! *Yesterday's Promise* is an uplifting read for today's faith-filled woman.

Tia McCollors
Author, *The Last Woman Standing*

God is calling His people to possess the land. He is anointing individuals to go into the "unique lands" of the days we live in to represent Jesus and proclaim the gospel of the kingdom. Vanessa Miller has an end-time, marketplace ministry to the fiction lovers of the world. I salute her for doing it in Jesus' name!

—Kimberly Daniels
Founder, Kimberly Daniels Ministries International
Pastor, Spoken Word Ministries

Acknowledgments

In 2007, I attended an event at which several authors were in one room, signing copies of their books. The lady seated next to me was a preacher who had written a book about women struggling to preach. Women preach at my church all the time. As a matter of fact, my bishop, Marva Mitchell, is a woman. So, I'd never imagined that women had any great struggle to preach.

Then, a man came into the room and walked over to this woman's table. When he saw the title of her book, he immediately started an argument with her. He didn't believe women should preach, and he was adamant about it. As I sat there listening to this man berate this woman of God, *Yesterday's Promise* began to take shape. So, the first person I want to acknowledge is Pastor Notoshia D. Howard of Indianapolis, Indiana. Thanks for sitting next to me at that event so that my eyes would be opened to the plight of women struggling to preach.

While I was doing research for this book, several women provided insight and scriptural knowledge to me. These women are either preachers or daughters of preachers, and I want to say thank you to Twilla Woods, Gwendolyn Coates, Kendra Norman-Bellamy, Sheilah Vickers, Christie Blackmon, and Donyalla Manns.

I would also like to thank my agent, Natasha Kern, and the author liaison at Whitaker House, Christine Whitaker, for believing in the project.

To my editor, Courtney Hartzel, and the design staff at Whitaker House, I can't thank you enough for all the work you put in to help ensure that *Yesterday's Promise* would be a success. I appreciate it.

I cannot forget to acknowledge the many book clubs and readers who anxiously wait for my next release. Thank you all for continuing to support my books.

And, finally, I would like to thank my family for putting up with me, my deadlines, and my tour schedules.

—*Vanessa Miller*

Dedication

This book is dedicated to all the women who have ever struggled to preach the gospel.

Know that God hasn't forgotten your labor of love. I salute you.

one

STANDING BEFORE THE CONGREGATION OF OMEGA CHRIS-
tian Church, Melinda Johnson preached a message on God's precious gift of salvation. Her mission in life was to tell as many people as possible about a
Man named Jesus. Preaching the gospel had become her
greatest joy. "Don't wait until it's too late," she told the
congregation. "The Lord Jesus wants to fellowship with
you right now. He loves you and desires only good things
for you."

Melinda continued in that vein until her voice cracked
and tears ran down her cocoa-cream face. She never tired
of talking about God's ability to do the impossible, or how
He could take nothing and make something miraculous
out of it. She usually avoided making public displays of
emotion, but this message was more important than her
image. As the tears continued to fall, she gave an altar call
and watched as dozens of men and women left their seats
and rushed toward the front of the sanctuary. Repentant
souls stood around the altar weeping as they raised their
hands in surrender to God. Melinda prayed to God on
behalf of each and every one of them.

After the service, Melinda stood by the sanctuary door
and shook hands with most of the people as they left the
church. This was something that her father, Bishop Langston Johnson, always did. Since he couldn't be there today,
Melinda wanted to make sure the job was still done.

"Thanks for your wonderful message, Sister Melinda," Janet Hillman said on her way out. "My son was one of the people who came down to the altar today."

For the past three years, Janet had spent her lunch hours in noonday prayer on behalf of her son. Having joined her on numerous occasions, Melinda was aware of the addictions and incarcerations that Janet's son had been through. However, Janet had kept the faith—she'd kept believing that her son would one day serve the Lord.

Melinda beamed. "You prayed him through, Janet. I should give you my prayer list, because I know you'll stay on the job until it's done."

When Janet walked away, Bob Helms, the head elder, came up to Melinda and said, "You brought down the house with that sermon."

"Thank you, sir, but I can't take credit. That message was God-given," Melinda said. After a short pause, she asked, "Do you know why the elders weren't at prayer this morning?" The church leaders met for prayer on the first Sunday of every month, but Melinda had noticed that none of the elders had been in attendance that morning.

"Your father had asked that all the elders meet with him this morning," Elder Helms told her.

"Oh," was all Melinda said. She had been with her father the night before, and he hadn't mentioned anything about meeting with the elders in the morning. The situation seemed odd to her because she had always been included in his meetings with the elders. Moreover, it was essentially understood by the entire church leadership that Melinda would assume her father's position once he retired. Right now, her father was in the hospital, recuperating from what he'd thought had been a heart attack. Now that Melinda thought about it, he *had* been given strict instructions to rest, which probably explained why he hadn't told her about the meeting. He knew that she wouldn't want him worrying about church business right now.

Elder Helms interrupted her thoughts. "The Bishop did tell me to make sure that you left church right after preaching the message, Melinda. He wants to see you immediately."

It seemed like Elder Helms knew something Melinda didn't, and it scared her. "Did something happen to Dad this morning?"

Shaking his head, Elder Helms reassured her, "No, no. Nothing like that. The Bishop is doing fine. He just wants to see you."

"Thanks for letting me know, Elder Helms," she said. "I'll head over there now."

Anxious to see her father and make sure he was all right, Melinda rushed down the hospital corridor that led to his room. He had been admitted to the hospital three days prior, complaining of chest pains. After several tests, the doctor had confirmed that no sign of a heart attack had been detected. Melinda was thankful that her father was recuperating and doing well. She was also excited to tell him about some wonderful, unexpected news she had received that morning.

Her father's eyes were closed when Melinda walked into his hospital room. As she approached his bed, she noticed for the first time that his hair was no longer salt-and-pepper but completely white. The wrinkles beneath his eyes, which had long made him look distinguished, were now more pronounced and distracting. *When did all of this happen?* Melinda wondered as she picked up her father's frail hand and pressed it to her cheek.

Bishop Johnson's eyes fluttered as he turned toward his daughter. "Hey, baby girl. When'd you get here?"

"Just a few minutes ago. I'm sorry I wasn't able to get here earlier."

"You had to handle my responsibilities at the church. Don't worry about it. I had plenty of visitors this morning."

Melinda sat down in the chair next to her father's bed and hung her purse on the arm of the chair. "I have some good news, Daddy. I've been asked to speak at the Women on the Move for God conference in August!"

"That's great, baby girl! But I have even better news."

Melinda raised her eyebrows. "What, the doctor gave you a clean bill of health and said that you'll live to be a hundred?"

Bishop Johnson shook his head and then blurted out, "I found you a husband."

"Excuse me?" Melinda said in as even a tone as she could manage. After all, she was a thirty-seven-year-old woman living in the twenty-first century. Fathers didn't go out and find husbands for their daughters in this day and age. "Please tell me you're joking, Daddy."

"No joke to it," Bishop Johnson said as he hoisted himself into an upright position. "I'm an old man, Melinda. I haven't got many years left. I'd like to see at least one of my grandchildren before I die, you know?"

Melinda couldn't deny that her father was showing signs of aging. But that didn't mean death would sneak into his hospital room and suck out his last breath while she stood there and watched. "You talk as if you'll die tomorrow."

"I could. The next heart attack could be my last."

Melinda rolled her eyes. "It was an anxiety attack, Daddy. Stop being such a baby. The doctor says you're fine."

Bishop Johnson shook a shaky finger at Melinda. "Now, you listen to me. I'm eighty-two years old. I know what's best for you, and that's why I called Steven Marks."

Melinda bolted out of her chair and moved away from her father's bed. She put a hand to her mouth and shut her eyes, trying to block out the same feeling of humiliation she'd experienced when Steven had dumped her ten years ago. *This has to be some kind of horrible joke*, Melinda thought. But her father was a serious man who rarely joked with anyone.

"Calm down. It's not as bad as you think," he said. "I didn't come right out and tell Steven I wanted him to marry you. He's a smart young man...he'll come to that decision on his own."

"Why are you even talking to me about Steven, Daddy? That man walked out on me and married someone else. Do you really think I'd want him back now, just because his wife is dead?"

"Pride goes before destruction, Melinda."

She really hated it when her father tried to rein her in by quoting Scriptures. "What does being prideful have to do with not wanting to marry a man who rejected me?"

"I have more to tell you. Would you please sit back down?"

Melinda inched back to her seat and slowly settled into it. If this marrying Steven Marks thing was supposed to be a buffer for the rest of her father's message, then she was truly petrified. She glanced at her father with a look of apprehension.

"This last hospital stay has convinced me that I need to retire."

Melinda rolled her eyes. "I've been telling you for years now to retire. I can pastor Omega, and Pastor Lakes can take over as bishop."

"Let me finish," Bishop Johnson said, holding up a hand to silence Melinda. "I know the ministry goals that you have. I also believe that there is a way for you to do God's will and also have a family. Plus, Steven's church did not support him during his grieving process. They want him to leave, Melinda. So, after prayerful reflection, I've asked him to take over for me as bishop."

Melinda must not have heard him right. He couldn't have just said that Steven Marks—the man who'd called off their wedding because she'd refused to give up her dreams of preaching the gospel—was going to be the new bishop of Omega Christian Church. In Melinda's mind, this could mean only one thing: her sin had finally caught up with her.

two

STEVEN MARKS WAS IN HIS HOME OFFICE READING his daily devotional when the phone rang. The caller ID displayed the name Langston Johnson. He picked up the phone and said, "Hello, Bishop Johnson! How are you doing?"

"Just fine, my boy. I feel like I could run a marathon."

Steven laughed. "Don't go running off too soon, or you just might end up back in the hospital."

"Thanks for meeting with me on such short notice this weekend," Bishop Johnson said.

"It was no problem. My situation here had been getting crazy, so I was home visiting my parents when you called, which made it easy to get to Baltimore."

Bishop Johnson cleared his throat, then said, "Well, I don't like beating around the bush. Have you made up your mind?"

"Did you talk to Melinda?"

Bishop Johnson grunted. "I sure did. I informed her that you would be taking over as bishop of Omega, and she told me that she would sooner set all twelve churches on fire than give them to you."

"She said that?"

"And much more. But don't worry about Melinda. She's headstrong, but she's still a woman of God. She'll come around."

"Do you think I should wait a little while longer before coming down there? Maybe Melinda needs more time to get used to the idea."

"I'm retiring at the end of the month. I need someone who is ready and willing to take my place now. So, are you going to be the new bishop, or do I need to call Pastor Lakes, as Melinda suggested?"

"I want the position, sir. I appreciate your confidence in me."

"That's good. I've already contacted the other pastors in the fellowship. I'd like you to come to town and meet with all of us next week," Bishop Johnson said just before ending the conversation.

As Steven hung up the phone, he wanted to kick himself for not calling Melinda himself. He should have known this would be a problem for her. He had grown up with Melinda. Years before they had dated, gotten engaged, and then called everything off, they had been friends. So, he knew she was hurting. If it wasn't for the fact that his daughter, Brianna, was also hurting, and that his church was throwing him out on his ear, anyway, he never would have agreed to take the position. But, more than that, Steven truly felt that God was moving him in this direction.

For the past ten years, Steven had lived in St. Louis, Missouri. Everything about the city reminded Steven and his daughter, Brianna, of his late wife, Sylvia. She'd decorated their house. She'd decorated his office and designed the pulpit area of the church. Even the local malls, grocery stores, and parks provided painful memories.

The car accident that had claimed Sylvia's life had occurred just two streets away from the church Steven pastored. He had to drive down that street almost every day to get to his church office, and, as much as he'd tried to forget, he still remembered how his heart had ached as he'd driven to the site, gotten out of his truck, and run toward Sylvia's car. A police officer had stopped him while several rescue workers had pulled Brianna out of the wreckage. The driver of the other car, they'd soon discovered, had been high on methamphetamine; he'd stepped out without so much as a scratch on him, and Steven had wanted to kill the man. To this day, he'd been ashamed to admit that neither his love for God nor the fact that he was a pastor had quieted his rage. Rather, it had been Brianna, who was five years old at the time of the accident. When the rescue workers had pulled her from the car and Steven had seen the bloody gash on her head, he'd forgotten all about his anger and started screaming her name: "Brianna! Brianna!"

At the sound of his voice, Brianna, squirming in the arms of a firefighter, had looked around until she'd found him. "Daddy!" she'd yelled back, lifting her arms to reach toward him.

The police officer had moved out of the way, and Steven had run to his little girl, taking her from the firefighter's arms and holding her tightly. Then, two paramedics had walked Steven and Brianna over to an ambulance so that Brianna could be checked out while the firefighters continued trying to free Sylvia from the car.

The driver's side been crushed like a soda can ready to be recycled, and, as soon as Steven had seen the crumpled car, he'd decided that he would never allow Sylvia to purchase another small car. Her Ford Escort had been no match for the solid frame of the Pontiac Bonneville that had slammed into it. But Steven wouldn't have a chance to discuss car choices with Sylvia. He would never discuss anything else with his wife again. He had known this the moment his wife had been pulled from the wreckage and her mangled body had been laid on the stretcher. Even as he'd run toward her, he'd been able to see that she was gone.

Now, he was trying to make life work without the woman who had brought him so much joy. His little girl was still miserable. He'd prayed countless times that she would smile as she always had before her mother had died, but, in the two years since Sylvia's death, Brianna had rarely smiled. Steven had taken her to meet with a Christian psychologist, but that hadn't helped the situation. She still suffered panic attacks every time he left town for a speaking engagement, mission trip, or other ministry-related event, to the point that Steven had refused to travel. The deacon board at church had determined that the decision violated Steven's pastoral duties, and he still didn't understand that one—it wasn't as if he had refused to preach at his own church.

However, the deacons hadn't let up. They'd also criticized him for all the time he'd spent away from the church during the first year following Sylvia's death. But Steven hadn't had a choice. He was both father and mother to Brianna now, and she came first. So, when Bishop Langston Johnson had called him to discuss his becoming bishop of Omega Christian Church, Steven hadn't been able to refuse. He recognized that some travel would be required of him, but he hoped that the change of scenery and the close proximity of his parents would help alleviate his daughter's fears.

His musings were interrupted when his office door opened, and Brianna ran to him. "Whatcha doing, Daddy?

"I was just sitting here thinking."

"Thinking 'bout what?" Brianna asked, climbing up on her father's lap.

Steven hugged his daughter. "Oh, I was just thinking how much fun you're going to have when we move closer to your cousins."

"And don't forget about Grandma Vicky and Grandpa Joe! I really liked spending the weekend with them. They bought me lots of presents."

Steven laughed. "I figured you liked that part of the trip. But when we move to Baltimore, you won't be getting presents every day. Grandma and Grandpa are retired, and they live on a fixed income, so I don't want you asking them for things. Okay?"

Brianna rolled her eyes as if her dad just didn't get it. "Daddy, I know not to beg. You taught me better than that. But, if they offer me some more stuff, I think it would be rude not to accept it."

Steven laughed again. His daughter brought so much joy to his life, and he thanked God every day that she'd survived the car crash.

"Daddy?"

"Yes, sweetie?"

"I know we're making this move so I won't be sad anymore, but I don't want you to be sad anymore, either. Okay?"

Steven thought he'd covered his sadness with laughter and smiles, but Brianna must have seen through his act. "All right, you've got a deal. Let's pray that God helps us to move past the sadness we've been feeling." They held hands and bowed their heads in prayer.

"Okay, now that you're out of the hospital, I'd like to have a reasonable discussion with you," Melinda said as she entered her father's reading room and sat down next to him.

Bishop Johnson set the book he'd been reading on the table next to him and put his hand over his heart. "I don't like the sound of this. Do I need to okay this conversation with my cardiologist?"

Melinda rolled her eyes. "Will you quit saying things like that? Your heart is fine. Everyone experiences anxiety, Dad."

"Does it put them in the hospital?"

"I don't know how many people go to the hospital because of anxiety," Melinda answered honestly.

"Well, I don't want to feel that type of pain again. That's why I decided to take it easy—so I can live long enough to bounce my grandchildren on my knee."

"That's the other thing I wanted to talk to you about." Melinda ran her hands through her shoulder-length, black hair. "Now, I can understand why you would want grandchildren, but what I can't understand is why you would want to make me feel guilty. After all, if you and Mamma had had more children, then you probably would have had some grandchildren by now."

The look of sadness that crossed her father's face tore at Melinda's heart, but she decided she couldn't let it get to her. There was too much at stake. "I'm not the only reason you don't have grandchildren," she continued. "So, I think you should cut me some slack."

Bishop Johnson looked at his daughter for several seconds before responding. "Your mother had a very rough pregnancy, Melinda. After you were born, her doctor cautioned her against having more children. Her body was just too fragile."

Melinda lowered her head in shame for making her father relive the pain of her mother's life and death. Margaret Johnson had been delicate for most of her life, and she'd had sickle-cell anemia, suffering her first sickle-cell crisis at the age of five.

During her pregnancy, she'd developed preeclampsia and almost died trying to carry Melinda to full term. Kidney failure had finally ended her life. Melinda knew one thing for sure: she didn't want to bring children into this world if they would have to endure that painful disease. "What if I pass sickle-cell anemia on to my children? Have you thought about that?" she asked her father.

"You've been tested numerous times, Melinda. You don't have the sickle-cell trait. Besides, Steven would have to have the trait, too, and I don't think he does."

Raising her hands in frustration, Melinda asked, "Why are you so set on seeing Steven and me get married?"

Bishop Johnson gave her a look that said he thought the answer was obvious. "The two of you belong together, baby girl. You may not see it, but your mother told me on countless occasions that you and Steven would end up together. She and Steven's mother spent hours on end planning the wedding."

"Why didn't you just tell me that you wanted me to marry Steven? Why did you have to give him the position you told me I would have one day?"

"I know you don't understand why I would break my promise to you, but I prayed about this, and I truly believe this is the direction God has led me in."

"Oh, so just forget about what I want, right?"

"If God wants something different, then, yes, baby girl, I have to forget about what you want."

Melinda folded her arms across her chest. "I don't believe God has anything to do with your decision at all. Don't worry about it, though. I'm used to broken promises."

When her mother had become deathly ill, Melinda had begged her not to die, and she had promised that she wouldn't. So much for that. Steven had also made her a promise that hadn't come to pass. Year by year, broken promise after broken promise, Melinda had learned to mistrust other people and their vows. God and her father had always been the exceptions; neither of them had ever made a false promise to her, and so she'd trusted them without question. She still held on to her trust in God, but, at this moment, her father had proven that he wasn't the promise keeper she'd always believed him to be.

"I'm sorry, Melinda," Bishop Johnson said with a sigh. "I don't think I explained myself well enough at the hospital. I truly believe that I'm following the will of God. I just hope I haven't scared you away from Steven."

"Don't worry about scaring me away—*Steven's* the one who's already scurried away from *me*." Melinda was getting extremely frustrated with her father. She didn't know how else to make him understand the way she was feeling than to come out with it. "Don't you remember the way he treated me, Dad? He broke off our engagement two weeks before the wedding."

"I remember it happening a little differently. The two of you sat in my office discussing your differences, and then you told him that you couldn't marry a man with such a backward way of thinking."

Melinda's eyes bulged out, and she lifted her hands as if her point had been made. "And what did he do? He left town and never looked back. He never even tried to work with me to resolve our differences."

"How could the man fight against God, Melinda?"

"He wouldn't have been fighting against God if he had just accepted the fact that I have been called to the ministry, just as he was. But that wasn't good enough for Steven. He wanted a woman who would open the door for him when he arrived home and wait on him hand and foot. That wasn't me then, and it isn't me now."

"Give him a chance, baby girl. The man has changed," her father pleaded.

Melinda stood up. "Steven Marks has not changed, and you know it. I can't believe that you are doing this to me. When he becomes bishop, that man will not allow me to preach. So, what am I supposed to do? Leave the church I helped you build so that I can do what God has called me to do?"

Bishop Johnson stood up and placed a hand on his daughter's shoulder. "No, Melinda. You don't have to leave. Marry Steven and work in the ministry with him. This is your destiny, baby girl. Don't you see that?"

Shaking her head, she turned to walk out of the room, then turned back to face her father again. "You, Mamma, and Steven's mother thought you had our lives all planned out for us. You just never considered that we have minds of our own."

three

WHAT ARE YOU DOING IN HERE?" MELINDA WAS surprised by her own harsh tone, but she'd been startled to enter the sanctuary and see Steven Marks and a little girl sitting in the front pew, looking toward the pulpit.

"Daddy was just helping me find the best seat in the sanctuary. I want to be able to see him real good when he preaches," the little girl informed Melinda.

"Bishop Johnson asked me to meet him here this morning," Steven said as he stood up.

He looked almost the same as when she'd last seen him—a little over six feet tall, and with a slender yet muscular build. His chocolate skin tone, light-brown eyes, and small, slightly crooked nose were just as Melinda remembered them. She watched him take his daughter's hand and begin to walk toward her.

As they approached, Melinda studied the little girl who held on to Steven's hand as if it were a safety blanket. She had a lighter complexion than Steven—high yellow, like her mother had been. But everything else about her was very much Steven. She even walked like he did, with her head tilted to the side, and favoring her right leg, so that the sole of her shoes would wear down on the right side first. Remembering this detail about Steven suddenly made Melinda want to scream.

The little girl tugged on Steven's jacket. He bent down, and Melinda heard her ask, "Who is that?"

"Remember how I told you that Bishop Johnson had a daughter, and that she and I grew up together?"

The little girl nodded, then asked, "Is she mad at us?"

Steven's eyes darted to Melinda, and then he turned to his daughter. "No, honey. Ms. Melinda's probably just surprised to see us."

"Then why is she tapping her foot and biting her lip like Grandma Vicky always does when she's too mad to speak?"

Melinda stopped tapping her foot and held out her hand. "You're Brianna, right? I'm Melinda. It's nice to meet you." They shook hands.

"It's nice to meet you, too. I'm sorry if we surprised you," Brianna said.

"I didn't expect anyone to be in the sanctuary, but you are a very welcome surprise," Melinda said, smiling at Brianna.

"You're looking good, Melinda. It's been a long time," Steven said.

Not long enough. Ignoring his comment, Melinda spoke in the most formal tone she could muster, "Well, I'll get out of your way. Bishop Johnson should be out to speak with you soon." With that, she turned on her heels and exited the sanctuary.

Inside her office, Melinda closed the door and leaned against it. Putting her hands to her face to stop them from trembling, she moaned, "Why? Why? Why?" She hadn't seen Steven in at least six years, and she'd hoped that, by now, he would have been bald and fat. But he still had a full head of wavy, black hair, and, from the way that navy blue suit had clung to him, Melinda knew that nothing but lean muscle would be found on the man. Meanwhile, she was ten pounds overweight. It just wasn't fair. Why couldn't God have afflicted Steven with baldness or a bowling ball gut?

Just then, Melinda heard a knock on her door. She rushed around to the other side of her desk and sat down in her chair. "Who is it?" she called.

The door opened slightly, and Steven's face appeared. "It's me. Would you mind if I talked to you for a moment?"

Shrugging her shoulders, Melinda said, "It's your world. I'm just taking up space in it."

Steven opened the door all the way and entered Melinda's office, sitting down in the leather chair in front of her desk. "Nice office," he said as his eyes scanned the room.

"It's small, but I like it." Other than the ministry, decorating was Melinda's passion. The moment she'd been assigned this office, she had painted the walls honey blush, put tan- and cream-striped wallpaper on the wall behind her desk, and hung burgundy curtains in the window to give the room a rich burst of color. Her bookshelf was lined with ministry materials, and the walls displayed beautiful photographs from her travels in foreign countries.

"Your father told me about the wonderful work you've done as Director of Missions and Community Outreach," Steven began.

"I'm sure he did. I'm sure the two of you had *lots* to talk about," Melinda replied.

Steven fidgeted in his seat, crossing his right leg over his left, then switching and putting his left leg over his right. "Look, Melinda—"

"Where's your daughter?" Melinda interrupted him.

He smiled. "She's still trying to find the perfect seat in the sanctuary."

"She seems sweet."

"She is," Steven said. He added, "She's been sad ever since her mother passed away."

Melinda nodded. "It'll take time, but she'll grow out of the sadness."

Steven leaned forward in his chair. "How long did it take you? You were nine when your mom died, but we never discussed her." With a look of confusion on his face, he asked, "Why didn't we ever talk about your mother when we were kids?"

Caught off guard by his question, Melinda crossed her arms against her chest, as if to shield herself from the memory of past hurts. "Umm.... Steven, I'm sure you didn't come in here to talk about my mother. Will you please tell me what you want?"

"Oh, yeah. I didn't mean to hold you up. I know that you're busy," Steven said as he squirmed in his seat a little more.

Melinda picked up a stack of papers from the corner of her desk and set them down in front of her. "I need to get my quarterly report to the Bishop this afternoon."

"Why do you call your father 'Bishop'? Doesn't that sound a little impersonal to you?"

Shuffling the papers in front of her, Melinda said, "I don't call him that at home. But, we're at church, and you are a business associate of his, so I'm just trying to speak with proper decorum."

"So, is that all I am?" Steven asked. "A *business associate*?"

How dare he insinuate that he's anything more? Melinda thought. This man had taken everything from her and then trampled on her heart. She wanted to scratch his eyes out, but she was determined not to lose her temper. He wasn't worth it. "What do you want, Steven?" Melinda made a sweeping gesture across her desk. "I have plenty of work to do, and I don't have time to entertain the Bishop's out-of-town guests."

Shrugging, Steven stood up. "I didn't come in here to upset you. I just wanted to let you know that I appreciate how important your position is here at Omega Christian Church, and that you don't have to worry about me getting in your way."

Melinda realized, with regret, that she'd lost the battle with self-control. She narrowed her eyes, figuring they displayed all the animosity she was feeling. "Thank you so much for not getting in my way while you're stealing my job."

"Come on, now, Melinda," Steven pleaded. "You don't expect me to believe that you wanted your father to appoint you as the new bishop?"

No, Melinda didn't want the bishop's position, but the way Steven spoke indicated that he'd think she was crazy to have even considered it. She stood up and gripped her desk. "I *should* be pastor of Omega Christian Church, and, if my father had done the right thing and made Pastor Lakes the new bishop, I would be."

"Did you ever consider that Bishop Johnson might have a good reason for appointing me bishop instead of Pastor Lakes?" Steven asked with just as much fire in his voice as Melinda had in hers.

"Oh, he had reasons, all right. None of which will do him any good. He'll soon realize that I'm not falling for his scheme. But, by then, it will be too late, and we'll still be stuck with you."

Steven opened his mouth, then closed it and took a deep breath. Finally, he said, "I'm sorry to have bothered you. I see now that this wasn't a good time." With that, he turned, opened the door, and walked out of her office.

If Steven lived to be a hundred years old, he would never understand Melinda Johnson. She was the prettiest girl in Baltimore—always had been, as far as he was concerned. That cocoa-cream skin, that long, flowing hair, and those unforgettable, hazel eyes had haunted his dreams for years. But Melinda had never been satisfied; she'd always had to have more. She'd had a successful career at Omega Christian Church as Director of Missions and Community Outreach, and her father had allowed her to preach there from time to time. But that hadn't been enough for Melinda. She wanted to be the pastor of this church, and, now, it looked to Steven like she was going to make his life miserable because she hadn't gotten the job.

Steven had known that Melinda wouldn't treat him with overwhelming kindness when he walked into her office. When they'd been kids, there had been times when she hadn't spoken to him for weeks because he'd made her angry. When Melinda finally would resume speaking to him, he would receive an earful and be forced to apologize for whatever she'd decided he'd done wrong. So, why he'd felt so compelled to go into the lion's den just now was beyond him.

"I found it, Daddy! I found it!" he heard Brianna yell as he walked back into the sanctuary.

He smiled as Brianna ran up to him, grabbed his hand, and proceeded to drag him up the aisle. "Okay, Brianna. Show me where you'll be sitting on Sundays."

"At first, I thought I would sit here," Brianna said as she pointed to the fourth pew back on the left side of the sanctuary. "But, then, I thought about the adults who stand up and wave their hands when you preach."

"That does happen, sometimes," Steven agreed.

Brianna released his hand, ran to the front of the sanctuary, and sat down in the front pew. "This is the best seat in the house," Brianna announced, turning her head to look all around the sanctuary. Then, more quietly, she added, "But if I sit here, people might stare at me."

A pang of anger flashed through Steven's mind. After Sylvia's death, some of the people in their congregation had begun pointing at Brianna and whispering to one another whenever she walked into the sanctuary. It hadn't been long before Brianna had refused to come into the sanctuary, choosing instead to stay hidden in a children's church classroom or in Steven's office. After two years, she still didn't feel comfortable entering the sanctuary when others were there. Recently, Steven had taken a week's vacation to give Brianna some time away from the church, and they'd visited his family in Clinton, Maryland. It had been during that visit that Bishop Johnson had called to discuss his position.

Steven had seen Bishop Johnson's retirement as the answer to his prayers. In Baltimore, Brianna would no longer be the little girl whose mother had died in a car crash just two blocks from the church. She would simply be the daughter of the bishop of Omega Christian Church. "I don't think you have to worry about people staring at you at this church," he finally told her.

"I know. But, just in case, I think I'll sit up there." Brianna pointed toward the balcony.

"So far away?"

"Yeah. I'll be able to see you real good if I sit in the front row, and no one will stand up and block my view."

Brianna probably thought she had Steven fooled when she told him she wanted to sit in the balcony so she'd have a good view of him. He knew the real reason: she was looking for another place to hide. Steven put his arm around Brianna's shoulder. "I'll look up at the balcony every Sunday and smile just before I begin my sermon, but I won't tell the congregation why I'm smiling. It will be our little secret," Steven said to Brianna. Silently, he prayed, *Lord, please give my daughter the courage to take the best seat in the house.*

four

WHAT ARE YOU DOING HERE?" MELINDA ASKED, holding the front door of her father's house open just wide enough to see out. When she'd peeked through the curtains at the sound of someone knocking, her mood had turned sour immediately at the sight of Steven and Brianna Marks on the front stoop.

"You keep asking me that same question," Steven replied. "What's wrong, Melinda? Does it really bother you that much to see me?"

Melinda caught the wary expression in Brianna's eyes and reined herself in a bit. It really wasn't her intention to make Steven or anyone else feel unwanted. She was still so upset about what her father had done to her that she was coming across all wrong. "I guess I just didn't expect to see you here tonight."

"Bishop Johnson invited us to dinner," Steven explained.

Still gripping the front door, Melinda said, "He told me not to cook. I figured he was going out for dinner." As she said those words, she saw a Brown's Catering truck pull into the driveway. Her father ordered from them when he was entertaining company, but he normally asked Melinda to call in the order.

"Can we come in?" Steven asked.

Melinda looked down and noticed that she was still holding the door close to her body. She opened it wide and put a fake smile on her face. "Sorry about that. Please, come right in. Have a seat in the living room while I get the caterers situated, and then I'll let my dad know that you're here."

"No need, Melinda. I heard the doorbell," came the Bishop's voice. She looked back to see her father taking measured steps from his study to the living room, where he greeted Steven and Brianna.

If he heard the doorbell, why did it take him so long to come out of his study? Melinda wondered. But she realized she knew the answer to that question. Her father was hoping that Steven would take one look at her and realize that he'd made a big mistake when he'd left her ten years ago. If it wasn't for the fact that she sometimes felt like she was watching her father deteriorate before her eyes, she would talk to him about his matchmaking scheme. But she couldn't bring herself to confront him right now.

She went to the back door to let the caterers into the kitchen, then showed them where to put the food. When they left, she opened the china cabinet and began taking out the dishes in order to set the table. This was Melinda's favorite part of dinner parties—bringing out the china. The dishes were cream-colored, with a simple, gold band around the edges. They didn't look like anything special, but Melinda's mother had picked them out. When she was a little girl, Melinda had helped her mother prepare for numerous dinner parties, and, years later, her mother had bequeathed the china to Melinda on her deathbed. Melinda had promised that she would always use the dishes for her own dinner parties and make sure nothing happened to them.

Carefully, Melinda set the plates on the countertop, then turned back to the cabinet to bring out a stack of teacups. Just as she was setting the fourth cup on the counter, she heard from behind her, "Whatcha doing?"

Startled by Brianna's voice, Melinda bumped one of the teacups with her arm as she turned around, knocking it off the counter. "Oh, no! Oh, no!" Melinda screamed as she lunged toward the tumbling cup. She fell to the ground, shoulder first, and the teacup hit her arm before rolling to the floor.

Now, Brianna was screaming.

Steven appeared in the kitchen and grabbed his daughter. "What's wrong?"

Brianna pointed at Melinda. "I made her fall," she said, starting to cry. "She's hurt, Daddy."

Steven put her down and knelt at Melinda's side. "Can you get up?"

"I hurt my shoulder, but I think so."

She accepted his help, leaning on him as she got to her feet.

Brianna rushed to Melinda's side and began chanting, "I'm sorry, I'm sorry, I'm sorry."

Melinda's heart almost broke at the sight of the frantic little girl in front of her.

Steven wrapped his daughter in a hug and said, "It's all right, Brianna. Calm down."

But she was still crying as she said, "It's my fault. I was talking to Ms. Melinda." Then, she started moaning, "My fault, my fault, my fault…."

"Shh, Brianna, please don't cry. I'm fine," Melinda assured her. When the girl continued to cry, Melinda mouthed to Steven, "What's wrong with her?"

Still holding Brianna, Steven turned her toward him, and she sobbed into his shirt. "Brianna was talking to her mother when the accident happened," he said quietly to Melinda. "She blames herself for it."

"Oh, no," Melinda said, her heart sinking. She knelt down at Brianna's level, placed a hand gently on her shoulder, and turned her around to face her. With the other hand, she reached up to wipe the tears that had drenched the girl's innocent face. "It wasn't your fault, honey. I shouldn't have leaped after that cup. I did a silly thing."

"B-but you c-could have died," Brianna stammered through her sobs.

"It still wouldn't have been your fault." Melinda rubbed her shoulder. "I'm way too old to be doing things like that."

Brianna wiped her eyes, then asked Melinda, "So, it was *your* fault?"

"Yes, of course it was," Melinda said.

"See, honey?" came Steven's voice. "Ms. Melinda was being careless, that's all. Her fall had nothing to do with you."

Brianna bent down and picked the cup off the floor and handed it to Melinda. "I'm still sorry I made you drop it."

Melinda sat down in a kitchen chair and studied the teacup, making sure that it hadn't been cracked or chipped. Out of the corner of her eye, she saw her father enter the kitchen. "It's safe," she said excitedly, then began rubbing her aching shoulder again.

"Why would you risk injuring yourself just to save a cup?" Steven asked her.

Annoyed, Melinda turned toward Steven and glared at him. "I wouldn't expect *you* to understand, Steven Marks. It has to do with a promise I made. And you don't know a thing about keeping promises." Not wanting Brianna to see her mounting anger, she stood up and walked briskly out of the kitchen.

"What did I say?" Steven asked Bishop Johnson, raising his shoulders.

Bishop Johnson pointed to the china on the counter. "It belonged to her mother. Melinda is very protective of it. She won't even allow the caterers to set the table when I have guests."

"Sorry—I forgot. I wouldn't have implied that she was risking herself for nothing if I had remembered that the china set had belonged to Mrs. Margaret."

Bishop Johnson patted Steven on the shoulder. "Don't worry about it. Let's just go sit down in the den until Melinda has finished setting the table."

As the two turned to walk out of the kitchen, Steven felt a tug on his pant leg. He looked down and asked, "What's up, Brianna?"

"I can set the table for Ms. Melinda. I won't break anything."

Steven's first thought was to say no. If Brianna broke any of those dishes, Melinda would never forgive him. But the look on her face was so hopeful that he turned to Bishop Johnson and asked, "Do you think that if we carried the dishes and cups to the dining room, Brianna could set the table?"

Bishop Johnson looked down at Brianna and winked. "Melinda was younger than you when she started helping her mother set the table." Picking up the teacups and saucers from the counter, he started toward the dining room. "Follow me."

Steven picked up the four dinner plates, then turned to Brianna and indicated the silverware drawer. "Can you pick out four forks and four spoons, sweetie? I'll come back to get the knives."

"Okay, Daddy," said Brianna, opening the drawer to take out the silverware.

When Steven returned to the kitchen, he found Melinda standing on tiptoes, reaching for a large bowl on the top shelf of the china cabinet. "Let me get that for you," Steven said. She stepped aside, and he grabbed the bowl from the cabinet, setting it carefully on the counter-top. "Do you need anything else?"

Melinda pointed to another large bowl on the same shelf. As he reached for it, she said, "Be careful."

The bowls coordinated with the gold-rimmed plates and cups, so they, too, were part of Mrs. Margaret's china collection, which was probably why Melinda kept the bowls out of reach and was now holding her breath and watching with her hands steepled, as if in prayer. At that moment, Steven realized that Melinda must still be grieving her mother's death. He wondered if she somehow blamed herself, like Brianna did for Sylvia's death.

He felt guilty for not doing more to help Melinda after her mother died. He wished now that they were nine years old again, standing on the basketball court at their neighborhood park.

> *He was holding his basketball when she walked up to him with her hands stuffed in her pockets. "Where you been, Melinda?" he asked her. "You didn't show up yesterday."*
>
> *She lowered her head. "My mamma died."*
>
> *He dropped his basketball. "That's awful. What happened?"*
>
> *Melinda picked up the ball. "I don't want to talk about it. Let's just shoot some hoops.*

That's the way it had been—years of not talking about the issues that concerned them. Now, as Steven watched Melinda make a big deal over her mother's china, he found himself wishing he had sat down on that park bench and hugged her until she'd been ready to talk. "Do you want me to carry these things into the dining room?" he asked her.

"No, thanks. If you grab the containers of food, I'll bring the platter and the bowls."

Steven followed Melinda into the dining room, hoping that she wouldn't go off at the sight of Brianna touching her mother's china. But, to his surprise, he saw Melinda smile to see Brianna placing a dinner plate on the table.

"Brianna, you did a great job setting the table. Thank you," Melinda said.

"It was no problem," Brianna said, grinning. "Your dad told me that you helped your mom set the dinner table when you were younger than me. So, I figured if you could do it when you were just a little girl, I should be able to do it now."

"Yes, and, at seven, you're much more grown up than Melinda was back then," Steven said with a grin on his face.

When they were seated for dinner and the mashed potatoes, green beans, and roast beef had been plated, Bishop Johnson turned to Steven after the prayer and said, "You know, I didn't make bishop until I was fifty-two years old."

"Yes, sir, I'm aware of that," Steven answered, slicing his roast beef into bite-sized pieces.

"In two weeks, I will be celebrating my thirtieth year as bishop. Melinda is planning a weekend celebration, and I'd like to end the event by officially naming you as bishop, and then having you preach the Sunday sermon."

Melinda put down her fork. "Dad, you can't do that. I already have a speaker lined up for that Sunday."

"Oh, yes, I'd forgotten," he muttered. "Will you give me his number so that I can call and talk to him myself? I'm sure Steven would bring him in to speak on another occasion," Bishop Johnson said, looking to Steven for confirmation.

"I don't mind bringing in a speaker you've already approved," Steven said, "but you may just want to have him go ahead and speak during your celebration."

"I'm sorry about having to cancel a speaker, but I can't think of anyone better to deliver the last sermon during my celebration than the new bishop of our fellowship," said Bishop Johnson.

Steven heard Melinda sigh, then say to her father, "That's the other thing we need to discuss. Don't you think two weeks is a little soon to have someone take over for you? Steven is hardly seasoned enough to step into this role without extensive mentoring."

"Melinda, do you really think this needs to be discussed in front of Steven?" Bishop Johnson asked his daughter in a stern tone.

"I apologize if I said anything offensive, Dad—that wasn't my intent. I'm simply stating that, just as I would have needed your help to step into the position of pastor of Omega, Steven will need much more help. He is not merely becoming pastor of Omega but becoming bishop of the entire fellowship."

Steven decided to take her side. "I would have to agree with Melinda on that, sir. I'm more than capable of becoming pastor of a church. I've done that for the last nine years. But I'm going to need your help in getting adjusted to this new role as bishop," he said, glancing at Melinda to see if his agreement had produced any positive effect on her mood.

She ignored him, her eyes fixed on her father, and said, "Dad, I would also like to request that you inform the new bishop of the fact that women are allowed to preach in *your* fellowship."

Steven turned to Brianna, who'd been listening intently, her eyes darting from one speaker to the next. "Ms.

Melinda and I have held differences of opinion concerning women and men preaching from the pulpit since we were children," he explained.

"Yeah, so, watch out, Brianna," Melinda said, eyeing Bishop Johnson. "Fathers have a way of stifling the dreams of their daughters."

"Not my daddy," Brianna proclaimed. "He says I can be anything I put my mind to." And then, as if remembering something, she said, "Well, except for a football player or a wrestler. Daddy says some professions are better suited for men."

Melinda smiled at the little girl's words. "I'm well aware of how your daddy feels about the differences in professions for men and women." She put her napkin in her plate, stood up, and then turned to Steven. "I'm sorry, Steven, but I'm not feeling very well right now, and I need some rest."

"Don't worry about us, Melinda. Brianna and I will just sit and talk with your dad," Steven assured her.

As Melinda walked out of the room, Steven was struck by a sense of sadness for her. He wasn't sure why Bishop Johnson hadn't kept his promise to Melinda, but Steven couldn't turn back now—not when he had his own daughter to worry about.

"I don't know what's gotten into her," Bishop Johnson said, shaking his head.

But Steven knew. Ever since they'd been kids, Melinda had believed that she'd been called to preach. And, ever since Steven's father had told him about the apostle Paul's instructions that women should be silent in church, Steven had opposed her dreams.

five

BETRAYAL WAS A HARD PILL TO SWALLOW. ALL OF MElinda's life, her father had told her that she was destined for greatness, and that nothing was out of her reach. He'd preached the same thing to his congregation, year after year. But, now, after being hospitalized for what he'd thought was a heart attack, he'd told her that she would not become the pastor of their church after all—not because she wasn't qualified, but simply because he wanted grandchildren. Melinda couldn't believe it.

Kicking off her black leather pumps, Melinda sat down at her desk at church and tried to focus on preparing the message that she was supposed to deliver at Bible study later that evening, but so many unpleasant thoughts were running through her mind that she just couldn't concentrate. Melinda had never thought of her father as a chauvinist; now, the thought couldn't be held back. Her father would not have denied a son the pastoral position simply because he wasn't married yet. She had half a mind to call Pastor Lakes and let him know exactly why he had been denied the position of bishop after all these years of thinking he was destined for it. Maybe she and Pastor Lakes could have her father ruled incompetent to decide who the next bishop should be.

Melinda stared at the telephone on her desk, wishing that she could betray her father as easily as he had betrayed her. She knew, however, that she had too much integrity and too much love for her father to do such a thing to him. But, she *could* expose the ulterior motive behind his decision. Maybe, if Steven knew the only reason he'd been chosen to preside over their fellowship was that her father had seen him as marriage material for Melinda, he would pack his bags and go back to St. Louis.

Melinda put her pumps back on, stood up, and strode out of her office. When she rounded the corner and approached her father's office, she saw Barbara Peters, her father's faithful secretary, seated behind her desk. Barbara smiled at Melinda and said, "Hello, Ms. Lady. How are you doing today?"

Melinda absolutely adored Barbara. When she'd been younger, she would pray that her father would marry her. Even though that had never come close to happening, Melinda had never lost her affection for the woman who had mothered her more times than she could count. She walked around Barbara's desk and kissed her on the cheek before saying, "I'm not having a good day."

"Are you still upset with your father for giving Steven the pastoral position?"

Melinda nodded.

"Have you talked to him about it?"

"I've tried, but he's not listening." Melinda sat down on the edge of Barbara's desk. "When did you find out he'd changed his mind about the leadership for our fellowship?" she asked.

"The day he went to the hospital," Barbara said. "He called me and asked that I set up meetings for him with the pastors of the fellowship and the elders of Omega."

"Why didn't you tell me?" Melinda asked, narrowing her eyes to hide the tears of hurt welling up inside.

Barbara put her hand over Melinda's and squeezed it. "Don't let this make you bitter, honey."

Melinda felt the tears bubbling up, and she quickly rubbed her eyes. "I'm trying, but this is so hard to accept."

"Do you want to pray?"

Melinda knew that she should be running toward prayer, but she hadn't thought once to pray about what had been troubling her in the past few days. "I'm too angry to pray right now," she admitted. "But will you please pray for me?"

"You know I will," Barbara told her.

"Thank you," Melinda said as she stood up and faced her father's office door. She knocked once, waited a moment, and then, hearing nothing, pushed it open. The room was expansive, and she had decorated every inch of it. She'd had the walls painted tan; the curtains and the carpet were a rich navy blue, and his leather couch and chair were a deep shade of burgundy, as her father favored these colors. The wall art behind his walnut-stained executive desk had splashes of navy blue, burgundy, and tan. It all went together to produce a strong image and a welcoming effect.

Yet welcome was the last thing Melinda felt when she looked at her father's desk and saw Steven sitting behind it, swiveling in her father's chair, while her father stood nearby, grinning like a proud papa. Melinda slammed the door shut behind her, and the two men stopped their discussion and stared at her.

"Oh! Hey, Melinda. I was just telling Steven that you would be willing to change the furniture in this office if he didn't like it," Bishop Johnson said.

So, now, her father was trying to highlight her decorating skills? Melinda was surprised that he hadn't asked her to cook dinner the previous night. That way, he could have sold Steven on what a fantastic cook she was. Rolling her eyes in disgust, Melinda decided to expose his motives before he could hatch any more matchmaking schemes. "Dad, do you really think that Steven will want to marry me just because I know how to decorate?" She looked over to see Steven's mouth hanging open at her statement.

Bishop Johnson stammered, "M-Melinda, w-what on earth are you talking about?"

Her father was giving her the eye, which was always a direct warning that she had gone too far. But, today, she didn't care. She turned to Steven. "Steven," she continued, "has my father told you the *real* reason he offered you the position of bishop?"

Steven gripped the armrests of the chair as he answered Melinda. "Your father was looking for someone with new and fresh ideas who could take the fellowship to the next level."

"*R-e-a-l-l-y?*" Melinda stretched out the word for every syllable it was worth. "And what new and fresh ideas do you have that will move our fellowship to the next level?"

"Melinda!" Her father's tone was one of reproof. "Aren't you teaching Bible study tonight?"

"Yes, I am."

"Have you prepared your message?"

"I'm working on it," she said. But, in truth, she hadn't studied her Bible much this week. That was something else she needed to pray about—if she would just go and pray.

Steven stood up and held up his hands like a lawyer objecting to a line of questioning. "What is she talking about?" When Bishop Johnson didn't respond, Steven turned to Melinda. "What are you talking about, Melinda?"

Melinda opened her mouth to tell Steven exactly what her father was up to, but a Scripture suddenly came to mind and caused her to close her mouth. It was 1 Peter 3:10: *"He who would love life and see good days, let him refrain his tongue from evil, and his lips from speaking deceit."* When she reopened her mouth, she said calmly, "I'm sorry I bothered you. I need to go work on my message, so I'm just going to leave now."

She turned to leave, but Steven's voice stopped her. "You can't come in here and say something like that and then just leave."

"I'm sorry—I've got to go," she said over her shoulder, then made her way out of her father's office as fast as she could. Opposing her father and Steven was one thing, but she was not willing to go against God. And Melinda very clearly felt the Lord telling her to be quiet.

"What was that all about?" Steven asked Bishop Johnson after Melinda had left. He moved around to one of the chairs in front of the desk, and Bishop Johnson sat down in his own chair.

When Bishop Johnson didn't respond, Steven persisted with his questions. "Is what Melinda said true? Did you offer me this position so that I would…*marry* her?"

Bishop Johnson finally said, "With the way she's been acting recently, how could I expect anyone to marry her?"

"But is that what you want from me? Is that the reason I'm here?"

"If you think that I would put my congregation and my entire fellowship in the hands of an unqualified bishop just so my daughter could have a husband, you're wrong," Bishop Johnson said. "If that was my only reason, I easily could have picked one of the two single pastors within our fellowship. They would have jumped at the opportunity to marry Melinda. But I've watched you over the years, Steven. You have a heart for God and a heart for His people."

"I appreciate that, sir. But do you really expect me to marry Melinda?" Steven asked again.

Bishop Johnson stood up and walked around to the front of his desk, sitting down on the corner. "A man should have a wife, especially if that man is a bishop," he said matter-of-factly.

"Ha!" Steven almost laughed. "You were bishop for twenty-eight years without a wife."

"Yes," Bishop Johnson said, "but I think I did Melinda a disservice. You might want to think about little Brianna. A stepmother could help her through these difficult years."

Steven pointed at Bishop Johnson. "Hey. That was a low blow."

"Look, son. The way I see it, you and Melinda were in love once. Who's to say you won't fall in love again?"

True, Steven had loved Melinda deeply at one time in his life. She'd been his first love. He'd thought it would be a forever love. But Melinda had been unwilling to compromise. "That was a long time ago, Bishop. Melinda and I are different people now. We want different things."

"If you ask me, the two of you want the same thing—to please the Lord with your ministries. That's a good place to start." Bishop Johnson shook his head and waved his hand, as if to dismiss the entire conversation. "I'm not trying to tell you what to do, Steven. Marry or don't marry, that's entirely up to you. And it's not something to decide on right now. Let's get back to work. Besides, I've got a retirement celebration to get ready for."

"Okay," said Steven, "but I need to make sure we're on the same page. I am bishop, whether I marry Melinda or not. Correct?"

"That's correct."

Steven breathed a bit easier as he and Bishop Johnson got back down to church business. But, later that evening, as he sat and listened to Melinda deliver her message about women rising up and taking their rightful place in the church, he felt he was witnessing another example to reinforce why the apostle Paul had exhorted women to be silent in the church.

Melinda was on fire tonight. She hadn't felt this much passion for one of her messages in a long time. As she asked the congregation to turn to Galatians 3:28, she felt a rumbling in her spirit as she read, "*'There is neither Jew nor Greek, there is neither slave nor free, there is neither male nor female; for you are all one in Christ Jesus.'*"

"Did you hear that?" she asked the congregants as they lifted their heads from their Bibles. "If God says that there is neither male nor female in His eyes, then why do many women continue to be denied access to the promises that God has made available to us?

"Turn with me to Acts 2:17–18." She waited for the members to turn the pages of their Bibles, then said, "Let's all read together." She looked down at her Bible and began to read, "*And it shall come to pass in the last days, says God, that I will pour out of My Spirit on all flesh; your sons and your daughters shall prophesy, your young men shall see visions, your old men shall dream dreams. And on My menservants and on My maidservants I will pour out My Spirit in those days; and they shall prophesy.'*"

She lifted her head from her Bible and said, "Now, I ask you—are we in the last days, or not? Because my Bible tells me that in the last days, sons *and* daughters shall prophesy, and that God is pouring out His Spirit on both men *and* women.

"I don't know about you, but a debatable interpretation of one Scripture telling women to be silent is not going to shut my mouth—not when I know that God has poured out His Spirit on me and has anointed me to spread His good news."

A chorus of women sang out, "Amen!"

"When you think about it," Melinda continued, "a woman was one of the last ones at the cross on Calvary, and a woman was the first one at the tomb. A woman was the first person to spread the good news of Jesus' resurrection. If it was all right with God to have some lowly woman flapping her gums all over town about Jesus, then don't come telling me that, today, women need to sit down and be quiet in church. Because, the truth of the matter is, if women stopped doing things at the church, the church would have to shut down."

six

As Steven listened to Melinda's message, he came to the realization that she was not going to take being passed over for the pastoral position lying down. But what she didn't understand was that he was not about to let her make a fool of him. He was here to stay, and he figured she had better get used to it.

When the service was over, Steven excused himself from a discussion with Bishop Johnson and a few of the members, then strode over to Melinda's office and opened the door without knocking.

Melinda was standing in front of her desk with her back to the door when he opened it. Steven had loved Melinda...once, he'd even wanted to spend his life with her. But, now, he just wanted to turn her over his knees and practice some tough love with a thick belt.

Melinda turned around and frowned at him. "Steven, I would appreciate it if you knocked on my door before barging in."

He had been rehearsing what to say, and he chose to come out with it, ignoring her comment. "Why would you disgrace your father and yourself the way you just did?"

Melinda put her hands on her hips. "I didn't disgrace anybody. You're just mad because I told the truth out there tonight."

Shaking his head, Steven sighed. "You are selfish and ungrateful, Melinda Johnson."

"Ungrateful? Well, what do I have to be grateful for?"

"For starters, you could try being grateful that your father created the position of Director of Missions and Community Outreach so that you would have an official job at this church."

With her hands still on her hips, Melinda made an exasperated expression. "I'm supposed to be the pastor of this church, and you want me to be grateful that I have a job as the missions director?" She shook her head. "You should have stayed in St. Louis and fought for what was yours instead of coming here to take what belongs to me."

Steven felt just as angry as she sounded, and, for a moment, he ignored the voice telling him not to answer hurtful words with more of the same. "Regardless of how or why I came here, the thing you need to realize is that I am your employer now, and, if you want to keep your job, you will learn to control yourself." He moved closer to her. As he did, he caught a whiff of her perfume. It was the same fragrance she'd worn when they'd been dating. He couldn't remember the name of it, but he remembered the scent. It was like a bouquet of flowers bursting full of femininity.

But Steven wasn't about to let sweet memories deter him from saying what needed to be said. "I will soon be the leader of not just this church, but also our entire fellowship. And I will not let you destroy all the work your father has put into building this ministry."

"He didn't do it alone, Steven. I labored right along with him, building this church into the megaministry it is today."

Shaking his head, Steven said, "You haven't changed a bit. You still need to have everything your way, or you'll go to war to get it."

"Oh, I've changed, Steven. I'm not as gullible as I used to be, and you can be sure of that."

Knowing what she was referring to, he took several steps back. They'd been eighteen and in love when it had happened. Neither of them had expected it, but they'd been about to head off to college and hadn't known when they would see each other again. They'd fallen into each other's arms, and, yes, Steven could admit it—they'd sinned. But when they'd graduated from college, he'd come back and asked her to marry him.

"I tried to make things right between us," he reminded Melinda, "but you would rather have preached than been a good wife to a man who honestly loved you."

"I could have done both, but that wasn't good enough for you," Melinda blurted out.

"Evidently, it's not good enough for any other man, either, since you're still single and your father is trying to find you a husband," came Steven's admittedly insulting retort.

He saw red-hot anger flash in Melinda's eyes as she pointed toward her door and said, "Get out of my office."

⌇

Things didn't seem to be going so well between his daughter and Steven Marks, and Bishop Johnson didn't know how to fix the situation. When he'd lain in that hospital bed praying to God, the fear that had been on his mind most often was that, when he died, Melinda would have no one. After his wife's death, he'd never remarried, so Melinda wouldn't have a stepmother or stepbrothers and stepsisters to lean on when he was no longer alive. Then, an image of Steven and Melinda dancing at their wedding reception had appeared in his mind. Bishop

Johnson had felt that God had been giving him a sign, letting him know that Melinda would not be alone when it was his time to meet Jesus.

He had been comforted by the thought, but he wasn't as comforted to realize that he might not live long enough to see the prophetic vision come to pass. So, he'd offered Steven his position and stepped down sooner than he'd anticipated. But, had he ruined everything for Steven and Melinda by trying to force the hand of God too quickly?

Suddenly, his office door opened, and his secretary entered, carrying two empty boxes from the stack lining the wall behind her desk. "Are you going to keep sitting in that chair and staring at the ceiling, or are you going to help me pack up your things?" she asked.

"Sorry about that, Barbara. I guess I was daydreaming," Bishop Johnson said. He stood up and took the boxes Barbara handed him, setting them on top of his desk. As he began to fill one with the photo frames from his desk and credenza, an overwhelming sense of sadness came over him. The reality of packing up his office in preparation for handing his ministry over to Steven was finally setting in. Funny thing was, Bishop Johnson knew that he would do it all over again if it would mean securing true happiness for his daughter. *Please, God*, he prayed silently, *don't let my sacrifice be in vain*.

He looked over to see Barbara wrapping up a painting she'd taken off the wall. "You may leave the rest of the paintings on the wall, Barbara. Steven wants to keep them," he told her.

Barbara put down the roll of bubble wrap and folded her arms across her chest. "Okay, spill it. What's wrong?"

Bishop Johnson raised his shoulders slightly. "Why do you think something is wrong?"

"I've seen that look on your face before, and I can tell that you're upset about something," Barbara said, moving an empty box off of one of the chairs in front of his desk and sitting down. "Don't think you can fool me and say otherwise."

With a sigh, Bishop Johnson lowered himself into the chair opposite Barbara. "Have you ever done something and then felt like you might have overplayed your hand?"

"Is this about Steven and Melinda?" Barbara asked, making Bishop Johnson marvel at her intuition. She knew him too well.

"I really thought I was doing the right thing, Barbara. I thought God was showing me that Melinda and Steven were going to get back together. But maybe I jumped the gun. I'm worried that I may have messed up their future."

"Why do you say that?"

"Haven't you noticed the way they treat each other? They can barely stand to be in the same room." Bishop Johnson shook his head in disbelief. "I know that God is not pleased with their behavior, but I feel like I'm the cause of it. What if Melinda becomes so bitter that she loses her way? What if Steven's anger towards Melinda stops him from becoming an effective leader?" He took a deep breath and then continued, "Don't you see, Barbara? I'm responsible for this fiasco."

Barbara leaned over and gently patted Bishop Johnson's hand. "Your heart was in the right place, Langston. You were just trying to do what you thought was right."

"But I'm destroying my daughter."

"That's not so. Melinda will be all right. She just needs some time to adjust to this. You had to know that she wouldn't be okay with your bringing Steven back here."

"She was in love with Steven once. I thought she would be thrilled."

Barbara shook her head as she mumbled, "Men." Then, she stood up and looked at her watch. "Well, you'll be my boss for only two more hours, so we need to finish packing up this office before then."

"Come on, Barbara. Don't leave me hanging," Bishop Johnson said, squinting and rubbing his temples, as he would if a strong headache were on its way.

Barbara sat back down. "Okay, you said that God wants Steven and Melinda to be together, right?"

Bishop Johnson nodded. "That is what I believe."

"Well, then, pray about it, get out of the way, and let God bring them together in His own timing."

seven

MELINDA WAS DETERMINED TO ENJOY HERSELF TO-night. After all, she had planned the entire event. Granted, she'd thought that it would be a celebration of her father's thirty years as bishop. Then, the next thing she knew, he'd flipped the script on her, and the event was to be a celebration of his retirement, as well. Now, she was no longer first in line for the pastoral position, and it seemed that, as far as Steven was concerned, she could either get over it or get another job. As if she would leave the church she'd helped her father build to the likes of Steven Marks!

She wasn't selfish and ungrateful, as Steven had said. And she was going to prove it. From this day forward, she would not fight her father on his decision. Not that it would do any good—his party was tonight, and he planned to introduce Steven to everyone there after announcing his own retirement. Steven would be installed as the new bishop during the church service the next morning.

Nearly ready to go, Melinda put in her diamond earrings and grabbed her yellow-beaded purse, which went well with the yellow evening gown she was wearing. It had a halter neck, with straps embellished with the same type of beads that covered her purse. Taking a final look in the mirror, she turned and headed downstairs.

"Wow!" she heard her father exclaim as she descended the stairs.

"You like?" she asked, turning around so that her floor-length skirt flared out.

"You look beautiful, baby girl."

She kissed her father on the cheek. "Thanks, Daddy." She was pleased with her outfit, too. She'd spent an entire week going from dress shop to dress shop, trying to find just the right gown for this occasion. She'd wanted this night to be special for her father and had done everything within her power to ensure that it would be.

"You are selfish and ungrateful, Melinda Johnson."

No, I'm not.

Melinda was determined to prove to everyone in attendance at tonight's event that she was truly happy for her father, and that she felt nothing but goodwill toward the man who would replace him. Besides, one of her best friends, Serenity Williams, would be there. Serenity had recently begun her own television ministry, based in Chicago, on the Word channel, and the show was taking off. Serenity wasn't struggling for the right to preach like Melinda was. Her family, including her fiancé, was very supportive of her ministry. Melinda was proud of her friend and wished her nothing but the best. But she also wished that she could enjoy the same encouragement from her family. Even though her father had permitted her to preach from time to time, he clearly wasn't committed to her continued participation in services. He knew as well as she did that, as bishop, Steven Marks would put a stop to it.

"Selfish and ungrateful...."

Clear your mind, Melinda chided herself. *This is your dad's night, not yours.*

And the night was spectacular. The catered food was excellent, the choir sounded like a chorus of angels, and the praise dancers were magnificent as they led the onlookers in heartfelt worship. Then, for more than an hour, people came up to the podium that Melinda had placed in the banquet hall to give tributes to her father. While one of the fellowship pastors was speaking, Steven walked over to Melinda. "You did good, Melinda."

On the tip of her tongue was a smart-mouthed response about the great things that selfish and ungrateful people could do when they put their minds to it. But, she had prayed many times throughout the day that God would give her a humble attitude. She turned to him with a smile and said, "Why, thank you, Mr. Marks."

Raising his eyebrows, Steven asked, "Why so formal?"

"In a minute, I'll be calling you Bishop Marks."

"No. Tonight is all about your dad. And I don't want to hear 'Bishop Marks' come out of anyone's mouth until after the induction tomorrow. Besides, Mr. Marks is my father."

Melinda turned to face Steven. The fact that he didn't seem to be in any rush to take the spotlight away from her father touched her. "Thank you, Steven. I actually spoke with your dad a few minutes ago. I can hardly believe he's seventy-six. He's bouncing around here like a forty-year-old."

"Yeah," Steven said with a chuckle. "He's trying to find all the members he knew when he and Mom attended Omega."

"Speaking of your mom, where is Mrs. Vicky?" Melinda asked, glancing around the room.

"She wanted to spend time with her granddaughter more than she wanted to attend the banquet, so she and Brianna stayed home."

"That's sounds like Mrs. Vicky. She was always more into her family than any activities at the church."

"And I loved her all the more for it."

"I bet you did. You were such a mama's boy," Melinda said, giving Steven a playful nudge. "It was always, 'I'm gon' tell my mommy this,' or 'I'm gon' tell my mommy that.' If I so much as bumped you accidentally, Mrs. Vicky knew about it."

Steven laughed. "She sure did, and she would have dealt with you if she hadn't liked you so much."

Melinda smiled. "I really miss your mom. I wish your parents hadn't started going to that church in Clinton, instead."

Averting his eyes, Steven said, "It was closer to their home."

Melinda knew very well that the proximity of the church to the Marks' home had nothing to do with their decision to leave. They'd left Omega Christian Church right after Steven had married Sylvia. Vicky had told several of her friends at Omega that she was ashamed at the way Steven had treated Melinda, and that she couldn't bear to stay at the church for that reason. But Melinda didn't want to rehash all of that with Steven. So, she simply said, "Well, I just wanted to thank you for allowing my father to enjoy his night."

"No need to thank me," Steven said. "I'm not interested in taking the spotlight off of Bishop Johnson. He's done so much for me, and the least I can do is give him this night." Melinda noticed a faraway look in Steven's eyes as he added, "He was my first pastor—the first person to teach me about Jesus. And he and my father helped me get through that terrible first week after Sylvia died."

Melinda's father had told her how torn apart Steven had been after the death of his wife. He'd even rescheduled his itinerary that week and asked Melinda to take over his responsibilities at the church. When Melinda had questioned why he was going to St. Louis before the funeral had even been planned, her father had said, "Steven is like a son to me. I can't let him go through this alone."

And her father had known just how alone Steven would be feeling, since he himself had lost a wife way too early. So, Melinda had let him go without another word. But she'd also sent up many prayers for Steven and Brianna that week. Seeing the sadness in Steven's eyes right now, she felt guilty for having neglected to pray for him and his daughter since the funeral.

"Hey, girl! You're looking quite lovely tonight," came a voice behind Melinda.

She looked over her shoulder and saw her beautiful, head-turning friend, Serenity. "Look who's talking! I'm sure every eligible man in the room stared when you walked in. And, speaking of walking in, what took you so long to get here?"

Serenity hugged Melinda. When they separated, she said, "Sorry I'm late. Michael stopped at a church down the street to talk to the preacher about a speaking engagement, even though I'd told him I wanted to come here straight from the airport."

"It's about time you got here! I was beginning to be afraid that you weren't coming."

"Girl, please! You need to work on your trust issues," Serenity told her.

Melinda hooked her right arm with Serenity's left arm. "Well, you're here now, and that's all that matters."

They started walking toward the tables when they heard someone clear his throat. Looking to the right, they saw Steven holding out his hand. "Hello, Serenity. It's been a long time."

"I would say so." Serenity shook the hand Steven offered her, then added, "The last time I saw you face-to-face, you were engaged to marry Melinda."

"On that note, Steven, will you excuse us?" Melinda didn't wait for a response and practically dragged Serenity away from him.

"What's your hurry?" Serenity asked with a giggle. "I was having a conversation with your new bishop."

"He's not a bishop until tomorrow, and you need to behave."

The two sat down at one of the tables in the banquet hall. "Okay, now. Tell me—what in the world were you just doing?" Serenity asked.

"What are you talking about?"

"Come on, Melinda. You know what I'm talking about. You were standing over there looking at Steven Marks like you had just come off of a monthlong fast and he was a piece of toast with grape jelly on top."

Melinda felt her jaw drop. She was caught completely off guard by Serenity's comment. She quickly recovered and said, "I was doing no such thing! We were just talking about my dad and how he'd helped Steven get through the loss of his wife."

"Oh, don't tell me you were letting that man cry on your shoulder—"

"No! It wasn't like that at all."

"Good. And don't let him weasel his way back into your heart, now that he's your boss."

Melinda rolled her eyes. "I'm surprised at you, Serenity. You normally have nothing but kind things to say about people. I'm the one who usually tells it like it is. What do you have against Steven?"

"I don't have anything against Steven. I just think he's directionally challenged."

"I hate to ask a second time, but what are you talking about?"

Serenity touched the palm of her hand to Melinda's head as if she were checking for a fever. "He didn't find his way to the church for your wedding, did he?"

Laughing, Melinda shoved Serenity. "You really need to stop being such a cutup. And let's not forget that he found his way to the chapel to marry Sylvia. So, he can't be all that directionally challenged."

"Yeah, but that's because Sylvia never had any ambitions beyond being a wife and a mother."

Melinda shook her head. "Be careful how you speak of the deceased."

"I'm not saying anything against Sylvia—I think it's a beautiful thing for a woman to take care of her husband and children. But Steven couldn't handle the fact that you wanted more."

"You just make sure that Michael can deal with your ambitions, Ms. TV Personality."

"Ms. Evangelist to the World," Serenity corrected. "And Michael is fine with what I'm doing. As a matter of fact, he encouraged me to sign the contract with the Word channel in the first place."

Melinda was about to respond when a woman on the serving staff stopped at their table, holding a tray with several glasses of iced tea. Melinda and Serenity thanked her as they each reached for a glass. When the woman moved on to the next table, Melinda said, "I hope he stays in your corner, because trying to do the will of God and the will of your man gets hard sometimes."

"Enough about me and Michael," Serenity said, taking a sip of iced tea. "How are you holding up?"

Melinda heard the compassion in her friend's voice, and she immediately felt grateful that, if no one else knew how she felt, Serenity always did. She was the daughter of a preacher, too, but she hadn't worked in her father's church. She'd chosen to follow God's lead to develop her own ministry. Now, her name and her ministry were spreading across the nation. Melinda sometimes wondered how far she would be in her own ministry if she hadn't stayed at Omega to help her father build his. Finally, she answered Serenity, "This doesn't seem fair to me. But, I've prayed about it, and I'm determined to see it through."

Steven was sitting at a table in the corner, watching Melinda and Serenity talk and laugh with each other. *They're probably laughing at me*, Steven thought. He regretted standing there like a sap, telling Melinda how much he appreciated her father for helping him through his time of grieving. But then, he reminded himself that Melinda would never laugh about it. No matter how mad she was at him, she would never make light of something so serious.

Steven put his suspicions out of his mind but quickly wished he could get them back. Because, now, feeling better about Melinda allowed him to focus on how wonderful she looked in that gown. After Serenity had said that Melinda looked lovely, Steven had wished he could have been the first to tell her that. He couldn't figure out why telling Melinda how good she looked tonight had seemed important to him, but that had been the reason he'd walked over to her in the first place. And then, all he'd said had been a lame, "You did good."

Steven wished that he and Melinda could work out their differences and become friends again. But could he just walk up to her and say that? Would she laugh in his face? Sometimes, when he looked at her, he remembered all the good times they had shared. His mother used to say that he and Melinda had fallen in love with each other from the womb. Their mothers had been close friends and had often gone shopping or out to lunch together while they'd been pregnant with them. When he and Melinda had started dating, Steven's mom had told him that she'd known it would happen because the two of them had never been able to stop talking to each other, even as babies. Life was funny, sometimes. Steven didn't understand how two kids who had talked to each other constantly could go for years without saying a word to each other and finally reunite, only to spend all their time arguing.

Why had Melinda considered preaching to be more important than him? He'd been totally up front with her when they'd started dating, telling her that he wouldn't marry someone who didn't think staying home and taking care of her family was a noble profession. And Melinda had assured him that she wanted nothing more than to be a wife and mother. As she'd gotten older, though, her attitude had changed, and she'd grown more convinced of her childhood calling to preach…. *Stop worrying about Melinda*, Steven ordered himself. He turned away from Melinda and Serenity and looked to the podium, where Barbara Peters was positioning the microphone in preparation to speak.

"I don't know where to begin," Barbara said. "I've worked for Bishop Johnson for twenty-five of the thirty years that he's been bishop of Omega Christian Church, and I've watched him build the fellowship into the awesome ministry it has become. All I can say is that I wish I could work with Bishop Johnson for another twenty-five years."

The devotion Steven heard in Barbara's voice told him that she would truly miss working for Bishop Johnson. He would have to remember to bring her some flowers next week or do something else to help cheer her up.

As Barbara finished, everyone clapped, and Steven noted how she'd managed to speak highly of the Bishop without letting on that this night was about celebrating not just his thirty years of ministry but also his retirement. That news would come later, when Bishop Johnson delivered the final speech of the night. He would stand behind the podium and tell the members gathered here that he was retiring; the rest of the congregation would hear the news at tomorrow morning's service, after which the Bishop would depart on a farewell tour to the other eleven churches in the fellowship.

But Steven was in no hurry for Bishop Johnson to stand behind that podium and pass the baton to him. The realization was just now sinking in that he was about to become responsible for twelve churches. After Sylvia had died, and he'd become fully responsible for Brianna, he hadn't been able to handle even his one church in St. Louis. But this was a new day, he reminded himself. With the help of God, Steven was determined to make this work.

"What are you doing sitting alone in the corner, my boy? This is a big night for you," Bishop Johnson said as he sat down next to Steven.

"No, sir," Steven protested. "This is not my night at all. I'm here to celebrate you, just like everybody else is."

"Well, you don't look very celebratory. You look like you're sulking over here in this corner," Bishop Johnson informed him.

Steven laughed. "Sorry about that, sir. I promise to smile for the rest of the night."

"All right, then," Bishop Johnson said, standing up. "Come on—we'll show these youngsters how to do a real Holy Ghost-filled soul train."

Years ago, Bishop Johnson hadn't allowed dancing at church functions. But, as the years had gone by and gospel artists like Kirk Franklin and Mary Mary had come out with up-tempo beats that Christians could move their feet to, a lot of churches, including Omega, had become more relaxed on the issue. But there was absolutely no slow dancing going on. "No bumping and grinding," Bishop Johnson always said.

"Yeah, let's show them how it's done," Steven said now, getting up to rejoin the party.

eight

MELINDA TOOK A SEAT IN THE BALCONY TO WATCH her father stand behind the pulpit for the last time as bishop of Omega Christian Church. He wasn't scheduled to preach this morning; Steven would do that. Her father would announce his retirement again for the benefit of those who hadn't been at the banquet the previous night. Then, he would introduce Steven as not just the pastor of Omega Christian Church, but also the bishop of their entire fellowship. Many of the people filing into the sanctuary this morning had no idea that an era was ending and a new one was beginning.

Melinda honestly didn't know how she would respond when her father made his announcement. Although she was thankful for the rest and rejuvenation his retirement would bring him, a big part of her was sad to see him step down; an even bigger part was still angry at having been passed over for the pastoral position. She wasn't sure if she would become a blubbering idiot or a mad black woman when her father announced his retirement; hence, her decision to sit in the balcony this morning. Whichever way her mood moved her, at least the whole church wouldn't see it. Her sole witnesses would be the few unsuspecting members and visitors seated in the balcony.

Her father had been her mentor, her friend. Until recently, Melinda had always thought she could trust him no matter what. In recent days, however, her father had been more worried about whether she would produce a grandchild for him than if she was following the will of God. *Why didn't Steven seem to care when I told him what Daddy was up to?* she wondered. *Why didn't he pack up, then and there, and leave town?*

Her musings were cut short when she noticed her father, the church elders, and Steven walking into the sanctuary and making their ways to the pulpit area. She smiled as she noted that her father was wearing the bishop's robe she had purchased for him. It was a simple, white robe with five-inch Latin cross monograms on both gold lamé panels and gold piping down the front pleats. Melinda thought that her father looked handsome, even at his advanced age. She'd often wondered why he'd never remarried after her mother had died. He'd told her that it was because she was the only woman he had time for in his life. But his rationale no longer held up, in Melinda's opinion, as he was expecting her to make time for a husband *and* a child.

Melinda's gaze drifted over to Steven, who was wearing a brown, three-piece suit with subtle, gold stripes. The long, lean lines of the suit were perfect for his tall, slim frame, and the white collared shirt and golden yellow, silk tie took the look up a notch. He reminded her of sunshine after a winter snowstorm. *Where did that come from?* she thought, quickly turning away from Steven to survey the elders, who were standing behind her father and Steven. Each one of the seven elders at Omega Christian Church was responsible for a specific aspect of the ministry, such as the School of the Bible, the youth group, and the "Senior Saints" program.

The Missions and Community Outreach program was the only program that didn't have an elder leading it. That was because Melinda had interacted directly with her father in its administration. Now that she thought about it, she basically had been performing the duties of an elder for years, but her father had not given her that title, either. The pulpit area was bursting full of men, but not one woman had ever been allowed to sit up there during a service. Well, Melinda sat up there, sure, but that was only when she was scheduled to preach.

Lost in thought, Melinda was brought back to reality when she felt an elbow nudge her in the side. Startled, she turned to see Brianna Marks sitting next to her, trying to get situated.

"Hi, Brianna," Melinda said quietly. "What are you doing up here?"

"I wanted to watch my daddy preach today."

"Yeah, but your daddy is becoming a bishop today. I would think you'd want to watch from the front row."

"*Your* daddy is retiring today, and *you* aren't watching from the front row," Brianna countered.

She has a point, Melinda thought to herself. "I didn't know if I would cry when my father announced his retirement, so I decided to sit up here and cry in private," she admitted.

Brianna leaned over and whispered, "I don't like for people to look at me, either. I told my father I would sit up here when he preaches, because the people at our old church used to point at me and whisper when I walked into the sanctuary."

"Was this after your mom died?" Melinda asked, her heart aching for the little girl.

Brianna nodded solemnly, then turned and looked longingly at her father.

Melinda sensed that Brianna really wanted to be on the sanctuary floor, where she would be as close to her father as possible. But Melinda also understood the trauma she'd endured at her previous church. The same thing had happened to Melinda when her mother had died. But Melinda hadn't let it get to her. Once, she'd walked right up to one of the pointing, whispering women and said, "You know, it's not polite to point at people. And it really isn't polite to whisper things, either."

The woman's face had turned ashen, and she and the woman with whom she'd been speaking had apologized on the spot. They had probably been afraid that she would tell her father on them. Melinda hadn't cared what their motivation for stopping had been; what she'd liked had been that word had spread around the church, and the church members had left her alone after that.

Melinda stood up and held out her hand to Brianna. "Come with me."

"Where are we going?" Brianna asked, her eyes widening. "I don't want to go into the sanctuary with all those people watching."

"We're going to my office. I want to show you something."

Brianna put her hand in Melinda's, then stood up and followed her away from the balcony area. When they entered Melinda's office, Brianna took a seat in front of the desk. Melinda grabbed a picture frame from the credenza and handed it to Brianna as she sat down in the chair beside her.

"She's pretty," Brianna said, taking the picture. "Who is she?"

"Her name was Margaret Johnson, and she was my mother. She died when I was nine, and I was really sad for a long time." Melinda paused, then continued, "When my mamma died, people used to point and whisper behind my back, too."

Brianna looked up at her with wide eyes. "Really? What did you do?"

"I told them to stop it, and then I sat right down in the front row and listened as my father preached. I learned a lot from my dad about being strong when I was a girl."

"My daddy wants me to be strong, too." Brianna lowered her head and added, "But, sometimes, I don't know how to be."

Brianna's honesty touched Melinda's heart. As a child, she never would have admitted that she didn't know how to be strong, even though that had been exactly how she'd felt then—and even now, at times. Suddenly, she had an idea.

When Brianna handed the picture back to her, she returned it to the credenza, then turned back to Brianna. "Do you think we could be strong together?"

"How?"

"Why don't we both sit in the front row this morning so we can watch our fathers up close?"

Brianna chewed her lip and tapped a finger to her cheek as she sat in silence. When she looked up at Melinda, she asked, "What if people point at us?"

"If anyone points at us today, I'll take you right back to the balcony," Melinda assured her. "But, after today, I want you to promise me that you won't let them get away with it."

"I'm not supposed to be mean to grown-ups. My daddy won't like it."

Melinda gently took Brianna's hand in hers and looked into her eyes—eyes that were full of sadness and pain over a loss that was too great to comprehend at any age. Melinda remembered how her own eyes had once held that same shade of sadness. Feeling an overwhelming sense of compassion for this little girl, she wanted to protect her and help her get through this difficult time in her life. "I'm not asking you to be mean to anyone, Brianna. You can very politely ask people not to point at you. But, if you don't think you can tell them that, just let me know who pointed and whispered, and I'll take care of them for you. Okay?"

Brianna nodded.

"So, can we go into the sanctuary and watch our fathers from the front row?"

Cautiously, Brianna asked, "You promise to stay with me for the whole service?"

Melinda held up her right hand. "I promise."

"And if someone points at me, you'll tell them to stop it?"

"I certainly will."

Smiling, Brianna said, "My daddy does preach really good messages."

"So does mine," Melinda said.

Brianna stood up. "Okay, let's go."

They walked into the sanctuary hand in hand and found space for the two of them in the front row. Once they'd settled into their seats, Melinda looked up to see that her father was now at the pulpit. He didn't hem and haw; he came right out and told the congregation that he was retiring. At the news, Melinda heard a collective sigh of disappointment arise from the members of the congregation. But Bishop Johnson quieted them, then started into a brief homily in which he reflected on his thirty years as the bishop of Omega Christian Church.

As Bishop Johnson was speaking, Steven rehearsed in his mind the major points of his sermon. *I can't forget to smile at Brianna before beginning*, he reminded himself. Then, he looked up toward the balcony to search for her. But she wasn't there. *Please, Lord,* he silently prayed, *keep Brianna from feeling self-conscious and wanting to hide.*

On the chance that Brianna had gained some courage and seated herself in the sanctuary, Steven scanned the pews. His gaze fell on Melinda, who was in the front row—and he nearly gasped at the sight of Brianna, sitting next to her in the very seat she'd called the best in the house. Her gaze fixed on Bishop Johnson, she looked completely at ease, and Steven said a silent prayer of thanksgiving. He was almost positive that Melinda had convinced Brianna to sit with her, and his heart filled with gratitude for the woman who had once held a very special place in his heart. At that moment, he found himself wishing that Melinda would let go of the past and give him another chance. But how could he ask her to do that after he'd walked away from her and married another woman? What did he have to offer her but another woman's child?

His attention suddenly returned to Bishop Johnson, who was wrapping up his speech.

So far, so good, Melinda thought. She hadn't shed a tear yet, and her father was almost finished speaking. "Now, I don't want you to be sad," Bishop Johnson told the congregation. "This isn't good-bye. I will still fellowship at this church when I'm not traveling. And Melinda will still be here, so I'll never stay away too long. Because, when I'm not missing you all, I'll be missing my baby girl."

He looked directly at Melinda, and she felt the tears coming on. "Thank you for everything you've done to help build this church. Don't ever think I didn't notice or appreciate all that you did. I love you, baby girl."

Sure enough, the tears Melinda had been afraid would fall started to cascade down her cheeks. She knew that her father loved her. He just didn't understand her God-given dreams. But she wasn't going to hold that against him today. Today, he was just her dad—a great man who was retiring from a long, fruitful ministry, a man she would miss hearing deliver the Word from behind the pulpit. "I love you, too, Daddy," she blubbered softly.

After Bishop Johnson announced that Steven Marks would be the new pastor and bishop of Omega Christian Church, two deacons stepped forward and presented Steven with the bishop's robe that Bishop Johnson had ordered for him, then helped him into it before returning to their posts behind him. As Steven approached the pulpit and prepared to begin his sermon, he found that he was too choked up to speak right away. Looking around at the many familiar faces in the congregation, he was overwhelmed with emotions. He also felt incredibly blessed; there weren't many thirty-seven-year-old bishops, and now *he* held that title.

Steven felt some of his composure return when he glanced at Brianna, who smiled and waved at him. Beaming back at her, he took a deep breath, then opened his Bible and addressed the congregation. "I want to thank you all for your warm welcome this morning. I know this change will not be easy for everyone, but I promise that I will do my best to serve you as well as Bishop Johnson did."

Steven spent the next ten minutes introducing himself to the congregation. And then, because he couldn't get away from it, he preached on the text of Luke 15:11–24—the story of the prodigal son. For, in truth, Steven felt like a prodigal returning home. He had gone through so much since he'd left this church, most of it in his determined attempts to leave Melinda behind and strike out on his own. Bishop Johnson had practically begged him to rethink his decision and stay at the church, but Steven hadn't been able to abide the Bishop's allowing Melinda to preach and promoting her belief that she was just as qualified as any man to pastor a church. So, he'd left.

And he'd become a broken man, having lost his wife and his church. His little girl had nearly been destroyed by everything that had happened. Then, Bishop Johnson had opened his arms and welcomed him back, just as if he'd never left in the first place. The mantle had been passed to him, and now, he was bishop and pastor of Omega Christian Church. Steven could hardly believe he was standing behind this pulpit preaching to a group of people he'd left behind a long time ago. As he finished his sermon, he looked at Melinda and wondered, for the second time in the space of an hour, if he had made the right decision when he'd left her behind.

He dismissed the thought as he stepped down from the pulpit, then proceeded down the aisle to the sanctuary doors, where he stood to shake hands with the congregants as they walked out of the sanctuary.

"Nice to have you back with us, Bishop Marks. I enjoyed your message," an elderly lady said as she stopped to greet him.

"I'm glad to be back, Mother Barrow." Steven recognized the woman the moment he saw her. When he and Melinda had been kids, she'd often given them candy as a bribe to keep quiet during the service.

She opened her purse and took out a peppermint. "You were good all through service, so you can have this."

Laughing, Steven accepted the peppermint from Mother Barrow. "Thanks, but I'm a little too old to be bribed with candy. You're going to have to think of something else to keep me on the straight and narrow."

"I know just the thing," Mother Barrow muttered with a smile, then walked away like a woman on a mission.

Steven shook hands with a few more congregants, who smiled and expressed their happiness to have him with them. Head deacon David Lewis came up to him and said, "I have the schedules for the deacon-on-call list, so, if you want to review the schedule for this month, just let me know, and I'll get you a copy."

Steven had met David the first week he'd come to Omega. Bishop Johnson had introduced them and later told Steven how faithful a servant he was. "Thank you, Deacon Lewis. I'll have Barbara schedule an appointment so that we can sit down and go over it," Steven said, patting David on the back before moving on to another group of congregants.

"We enjoyed your message, Bishop Marks. Glad to have you with us," one of the men in the group said.

As Steven made his way to another group, he saw Mother Barrow rushing toward him, pulling Melinda behind her.

He chuckled to conceal his mild alarm. "I thought you'd left already, Mother Barrow."

"Not yet," Mother Barrow said, pushing Melinda forward until she was right in front of Steven. "I found just the person to keep you in line."

nine

THE CHURCH OFFICE WAS CLOSED ON MONDAYS, AS the staff was always on call during Sunday services. When Melinda walked into the church on Tuesday, the first day when her father would not be in the office with her, she felt uneasy, as if she didn't belong at this church anymore.

Everything about the building was the same—everything except for the fact that her father was now five hundred miles away, traveling from church to church on his farewell tour. Melinda wanted to be with him, but her job was here...with Steven. She still didn't like the idea of working for her ex-fiancé, and she wasn't sure what her father had been thinking when he'd made his decision. Of course, she understood that he'd had marriage on his mind, but she'd made it perfectly clear that Steven was the last man she would ever consider marrying. So, why hadn't her father backed down?

She couldn't concentrate. All morning long, she kept thinking about the congregation's response to Steven. She didn't know for sure if she had been hoping for a mass protest when her father announced that Steven would be the new pastor instead of her, but when no one had become noticeably upset or even seemed to be aware that she had been slighted, she'd begun to wonder if her ministry at this church had ever really mattered to anyone else. Maybe the members who had told her that her sermons were great, that she was doing a wonderful job as

Director of Missions and Community Outreach, had done so because her father had been the bishop and not at all because they'd believed it.

Attempting to focus on other things, Melinda signed online, hoping to find responses to several e-mails she'd sent out last week. But when she checked her inbox, she found that no one had responded to her. All of her new messages amounted to junk mail. She deleted a long string of them and was about to sign off when she noticed a new e-mail with a subject line that read, "We don't want you here." She didn't recognize the sender, but curiosity made her click on it, anyway.

The message was brief: "Stop causing trouble and realize that no one at this church wants you as the pastor. God will judge you and all the rest of the women in this world who go against His will."

Melinda stared at the screen, wondering why someone would send her such a menacing message. She hadn't said anything to her father or Steven about the pastoral position in days. Her father had left town two hours after the service on Sunday, and she hadn't seen Steven since Sunday, either. So, how could she have been "causing trouble"? Then, it hit her. Her father wasn't here to protect her anymore, and Steven was trying to run her out of a ministry she'd helped build. Anger began to overtake her as she printed out the e-mail, then marched out of her office, document in hand.

"What's the matter?" Barbara Peters asked when Melinda stomped into her office.

"Is he in?" Melinda asked, pointing at Steven's door.

"Yes, honey, he's in. But I need you to come and sit with me so you can calm down before going in there, okay?"

Tears stung Melinda's eyes as she admitted, "I don't want to calm down, Barbara. I want to tell Steven exactly what I think of him."

Barbara stood up and came out from behind her desk to pull Melinda into her arms. "Don't do this to yourself, honey. I know life doesn't seem fair right now, but God will turn this around for you. Just wait and see."

"He doesn't want me here, Barbara. He doesn't want me here," Melinda sobbed as Barbara held her.

Suddenly, Steven's office door opened. "What's going on out here?" he asked.

Melinda pulled away from Barbara's embrace and held up the e-mail in Steven's face. "Is this your doing?"

"Hello to you, too, Melinda," Steven said.

"Don't you hello me." She pointed at the paper. "Did you have anything to do with this?"

Steven squinted to read the message, then looked up at Melinda and said, "Will you come into my office?" She sighed and followed him in, shutting the door behind her.

"I don't understand why you think I had something to do with this e-mail," he began.

Her hands on her hips, Melinda said, "Oh, don't play coy with me, Steven. We both know that you have never wanted me to preach."

"That doesn't mean I would send something that mean to you. Believe it or not, Melinda, I do care about your feelings."

"Oh, yeah, I'm *sure* you do," Melinda said.

"What's that supposed to mean?" Steven asked, leaning against his desk and folding his arms across his chest. "You act as if I'm out to get you or something."

Giving him a scornful look, she spat out, "No, I think you've gotten everything you ever wanted from me."

Looking deflated, Steven lowered his gaze to the floor. Melinda knew she had him right where she wanted him. What could he say? In a moment of youthful lust, he'd taken her virginity, and now, years later, he had taken the position she'd waited for her whole life.

Finally, still looking at the floor, he said, "I have a lot of work to do today, Melinda. So, can you please let me get back to it?"

How dare he dismiss her like she was a petty child he could no longer tolerate? Melinda straightened to her full five-feet-seven height. Her shoulders stiffened as she said, "All right, Bishop Marks. I will take my petty issues back to my office and let you get back to more important things."

"That's not what I meant."

Melinda wasn't listening. She turned away from Steven and stormed out of his office in a worse mood than she'd been in when she'd gone into it. Seeing an empty box in the hallway, probably discarded after Steven's move, she picked it up and took it back to her office. She slammed the box on her desk and looked around the room, wondering what she should pack first. Photos? Books?

Suddenly, a knock on her door interrupted her task. She turned to see Darlene Scott, the office manager, open the door and walk in. Melinda liked Darlene—they both were single and around the same age. They occasionally went out to lunch together, but that was about the extent of their friendship.

"What's going on? Are you okay?" Darlene asked, closing the door behind her.

"Yeah," Melinda grumbled, taking the box off her desk and setting it on the floor. Feeling her anger subsiding, she sat down in her chair.

"What's the box for?" Darlene asked.

"I was getting ready to pack my things and get out of here."

"Why would you do that? Because you helped your father build this church, and he's no longer here?"

"It's not just that." Melinda nodded in the direction of Steven's office. "*He* doesn't want me here."

Darlene sat down across from Melinda. "Did Bishop Marks say that?"

Melinda shook her head. "He didn't have to say it. I just know."

"Well, since he didn't say it, do you think you can stay employed here long enough to meet with Billy Woods?"

Melinda stood up and grabbed her calendar off her desk, then looked back at Darlene with a guilty expression on her face. "I'd forgotten all about the appointment I'd set up with Billy. Yes, please send him in immediately."

"I will. But, first," Darlene said, standing up and holding out her hands to Melinda, "you need to pray. You're not in the right frame of mind to meet with a juvenile delinquent."

Melinda put her hands in Darlene's and bowed her head. When Darlene had finished praying, Melinda felt as if a weight had been lifted, and she appreciated the gesture all the more. "Thanks, Darlene. You're a true friend."

"I try to be. Now, just relax, okay?"

"I can't," Melinda said with a laugh. "You're about to send Billy in here!"

"Do you still have that taser I bought you?" Darlene asked.

Melinda opened her middle desk drawer. "Right here. But I won't need it. Billy didn't come here for a fight."

"I hope you're right," Darlene said with a wink, then walked out the door.

Melinda sat down at her desk and waited for Billy Woods to come in. For more than a year, she had led a group of evangelists on regular walks through Billy's neighborhood, passing out gospel tracts and praying with every person who would let them. The area had been crawling with drug dealers, including seventeen-year-old Billy Woods.

When Melinda had first met him, Billy had threatened her with bodily harm if she didn't clear her "Jesus freaks" out of his neighborhood. On a later occasion, he'd told her, "Ain't none of us interested in crossing over, so you might as well get outta here."

Melinda had politely refused to leave, then had gone a step further and invited Billy and his friends to a cookout and Christian rock concert event at the church. Billy had laughed at her, but he'd shown up at the cookout. And, ever since then, he and Melinda had conversed in friendly terms whenever they'd seen each other. Melinda had always asked him, "So, are you interested in crossing over now?" and, every time, Billy had just laughed.

Then, Melinda had met Billy's mother. Brenda Woods worked two jobs to support herself and her son. She'd told Melinda that Billy had been an A and B student until his father had left them, about six months prior to Melinda's meeting her. Brenda had feared losing Billy to the streets but hadn't had the time to keep him in line because she'd been working constantly just to keep a roof over their heads.

Billy also had been an outstanding basketball player. He'd been on the basketball team at his high school and had been set to receive a scholarship, but when his father had left, he'd gotten into drugs and had been kicked off the team. Brenda had been doing everything she could think of to get Billy back on track, but nothing had worked. She'd reached her wit's end but still had been determined that her son would not become a statistic. It had been then that she'd turned to Melinda for help. "Take him to church with you," she'd begged.

When Melinda had explained that he'd refused her many previous invitations to church, Brenda had said, "Force him to go."

This had made Melinda raise her eyebrows and say, "Your son is six feet seven inches. I can't force him to go anywhere."

"If you come pick him up this Sunday morning, I guarantee that he'll get in that car with you," Brenda had said.

And, true to her word, Brenda had made sure that Billy had been dressed and ready for church when Melinda had pulled up in front of their apartment building. The following week, Billy had come to church on his own. At this point, he hadn't yet confessed Jesus Christ as Savior—he hadn't "crossed over," as he called it. But he'd been getting closer.

Three months ago, Billy had confided in Melinda that he'd been thinking about going to college. Melinda had helped enroll him in a night school program so that he could make up some of the credit hours he'd been missing, and then had helped him with his college applications. She'd scheduled today's appointment with Billy to make sure that he was staying on track.

"Hey, Lady J," Billy said as he walked through her door, closed it behind him, and sat down in a chair.

"Hey, Mr. W," she answered back, referring to him by the first initial of his last name, just as he did when addressing most people.

"I've got some good news," he said, fishing a folded piece of paper from his pocket. "I was accepted at the University of Maryland."

"Woo-hoo! Way to go!" Melinda jumped up from her seat, rounded her desk, and gave Billy a hug. "That's wonderful news. I'm so excited for you!"

"Me, too," Billy said. Then, he laid another shocker on her. "I went down to the school and tried out for the basketball team, since I'd missed the recruitment period. Funny thing about it was, Coach Wilkinson acted like he knew all about me."

Melinda couldn't help but smile. "He's on Twitter, so I sent him a few tweets about how fabulous you are," she confessed.

"No wonder he was so nice to me! I don't know what all you said, Lady J, but I think I'm on the team."

Suddenly, Billy wrapped her in a bear hug, picked her up, and began swinging her around. "Put me down!" Melinda squealed, laughing all the while.

"Thank you, thank you, thank you," Billy said as he continued swinging her around.

Melinda was getting dizzy. "Okay, Billy. You can put me down now."

Just as Billy was slowing his spins, the door to her office burst open, and Steven charged in. "Put her down right now," he demanded of the youth, who stood five inches taller than he.

When Melinda's feet hit the floor, Billy still had his arm around her shoulders.

Steven took a step forward. "Take your hands off her."

Breathless, Melinda tried to wave off Steven's worries as she struggled to inhale and exhale. Finally, she caught her breath enough to say, "It's okay, Steven. Billy and I were in the middle of a meeting."

"This is how you conduct meetings at the church?" Steven asked through gritted teeth.

Melinda noticed that Billy's arm was still around her shoulders. She moved away from him and straightened her suit jacket, then glared at Steven. "I'm not sure what you are trying to insinuate, Steven, but kindly get your mind out of the gutter and let me finish my meeting. Please."

Steven folded his arms across his chest and looked at Billy. "I'm not sure I should leave the two of you alone in here."

"I wasn't trying to do anything to Lady J," Billy protested. "I was just excited about getting accepted into college and possibly getting a spot on the basketball team."

"It's okay, Billy," Melinda said. "You haven't done anything wrong. Bishop Marks was just worried because he doesn't know you." She looked at Steven. "Steven, this is Billy Woods. He's a senior at Thurgood Marshall High, and he's just been accepted at the University of Maryland." She then turned to Billy and said, "Billy, this is Steven Marks, the new bishop and pastor of Omega."

Steven cleared his throat and extended a hand to Billy. "Nice to meet you, young man."

"Thanks, sir," Billy said, shaking his hand. "It's nice to meet you, too. I was at church when you preached about being the prodigal son. That was deep."

"Thanks," Steven said. "I'm glad it resonated with you."

Enough schmoozing, Melinda thought. "Can I please get back to my meeting now, Steven?" she asked.

Steven relented. "Fine, I'll leave. But I want this door left wide open."

"For goodness' sake, Steven. Billy is half my age. Do you really think he wants to carry on with someone who could be his mother?"

"He's a teenage boy, isn't he?" Steven responded, pausing at the door.

Raising her eyebrows, Melinda asked, "And what's that supposed to mean?"

"It means…. Just leave the door wide open," Steven finally said, then turned and walked down the hall.

When Melinda looked over at Billy, he had a big grin on his face. "What are you laughing about?"

"Dude's got it bad," Billy said, still smirking.

"Hush up, Billy. You don't know what you're talking about," Melinda said, sitting down again at her desk.

"Seriously, that dude was ready to take my head off about you. And he has to be at least forty. I could beat him to a pulp."

"Yeah, forty is real old, isn't it?" Melinda said, glaring good-humoredly at Billy.

He held up his hands. "No disrespect. Just making an observation."

"Well, observe somebody other than that 'dude,' because he isn't thinking about me," Melinda assured him.

Shaking his head, Billy muttered, "You must be blind."

The last thing Melinda wanted to do was analyze Steven's motives for doing anything. She had given up trying to figure him out a long time ago. Reaching across her desk, she told Billy, "Here, give me your acceptance letter so that I can pray over it."

"It's too late to pray, Lady J. I already have the acceptance letter."

"Boy, hand me that letter," she said. "It's never too late to pray."

ten

AFTER HER MEETING WITH BILLY WOODS AND THE EN-
counter with Steven, Melinda went home and
studied her Bible. She recognized that she'd been
becoming increasingly angry and bitter, and she didn't like
that at all. Whenever she was writing a sermon, Melinda
used her concordance to find Scriptures that related to the
subject she was speaking about. When she was reading the
Bible for personal study, though, Melinda prayed and then
opened the Book, trusting that God would lead her to the
Scriptures He wanted her to study. The first verse she read
that afternoon was Ephesians 4:26: *"Be angry, and do not
sin': do not let the sun go down on your wrath."*

She felt immediately convicted; the sun had set and
risen a number of times since she'd gotten angry at Steven, and she was still angry. "Okay, Lord," she prayed. "I
know that You are not pleased with my attitude. But I
need Your help to fix it. I believe that You have called me
to preach, but if You allow Steven to preside over our fellowship, I fear I may never get another chance."

Returning to the Word, she flipped back and found
herself in the book of Proverbs. Her eyes settled on
Proverbs 3:5-6: *"Trust in the LORD with all your heart, and
lean not on your own understanding; in all your ways
acknowledge Him, and He shall direct your paths."*

Melinda hugged her Bible to her chest. The words she'd
just read were so refreshing. They told her that she didn't

have to worry about the decisions her father and Steven had made, or how they were affecting her, because, if she trusted God and acknowledged Him, He would show her which way to go. She resumed her prayer: "Lord, I love You, and I truly want to please You. So, please guard my tongue and renew my heart with the right spirit as I go to work tomorrow. In Your Son's name, amen."

The next morning, Melinda stopped at the local florist on her way to the church to pick up two bouquets of Gerber daisies—one for Barbara Peters, the other for Darlene Scott. Ever since her father had given the pastoral position to Steven, Melinda had not been herself, and she definitely hadn't been treating others as she wanted to be treated. She decided to stop that trend today.

"What are these for?" Darlene asked, taking the daisies from Melinda and inhaling their fragrance.

"To thank you for putting up with me the past few days," Melinda said. "I want to apologize for the way I've been acting lately."

Darlene stood up and hugged Melinda. "Girl, you don't have to apologize to me. I've worked with you for years. I know what kind of heart you have."

"Thanks for saying that, Darlene. But I know I've been acting like a crazy lady. And I'm sorry about that."

"Okay, okay, I accept your apology. Now, get out of here before you make me cry."

Melinda laughed to herself as she turned the corner, but she stopped abruptly when she heard a commotion coming from her office. She opened the door stealthily, then smiled with relief to see Brianna swiveling around in her chair. "What are you doing in here, munchkin?"

Brianna stopped the chair in mid-rotation and smiled at Melinda. "I wanted to see you before I went to school."

"Oh, really? What for?"

Brianna jumped out of the chair, ran over to Melinda, and gave her a big hug. "I wanted to give you a hug all day yesterday, but Daddy wouldn't take me over to your house," Brianna told her.

Melinda could have used a hug the previous day, and she gladly would have accepted one from Brianna. The little girl's kindness seemed to soften Melinda's heart a bit more each time she came in contact with her. "You're so sweet, Brianna. How did you know that a hug was exactly what I needed?"

"Everybody needs hugs."

"There you are," Steven said as he peeked into Melinda's office. "Didn't I tell you not to bother Ms. Melinda today?"

"Ms. Melinda doesn't mind," Brianna told her father, then looked up at Melinda. "Do you?"

Seeing Brianna stare at her with those big, beautiful, brown eyes, Melinda couldn't say anything but, "Of course, I don't mind. You can bother me any day you want, if it means I'll get a hug."

Brianna giggled. "See, Daddy? I *told* you she wouldn't mind." She gave Melinda another hug and then added, "You feel just like my mom."

"Okay, Brianna," Steven announced with an air of urgency. "We need to get you to school!"

"Bye, Ms. Melinda," Brianna said, waving behind her as she walked out of the office and followed her father down the hall.

Melinda waved after her, then sat down at her desk and tried to get Brianna's comment out of her mind. Why did she have to bring up her mother? Even as she asked the question, though, Melinda understood the answer. After her mother had died, she'd hugged aunts, neighbors, friends' mothers, and female church members, hoping to get back the feeling she'd had when hugging her own mother. But no one's hug had ever compared. *"You feel just like my mom."*

Melinda picked up a stack of papers and started leafing through them. *Just get to work*, she told herself. *You're not Brianna's mother, and you never will be.*

After dropping Brianna off at school, Steven returned to his office and tried to concentrate, but his daughter's words kept floating through his mind. *"You feel just like my mom."* He'd thought that Brianna would eventually get over the loss of her mother, but he was starting to fear that she would never get past it unless he found her another mother. But what was he supposed to do? It wasn't as if there was a store where he could go to pick up the perfect second mommy to help Brianna heal from the pain of losing her first mommy.

A mountain of files covered Steven's desk, so he really didn't have time to dwell on the situation with Brianna right now. One of the files had to do with the mission trip Melinda was planning to Uganda this year. Steven picked up his phone and dialed Darlene's extension. When she answered, he said, "Hello, Darlene. How are you today?"

"I'm doing good, Bishop Marks. What can I do for you?"

"Can you please ask Melinda to come to my office when she has a moment?"

"Sure, I'll do that," Darlene assured him. "Oh, and, Bishop Marks? It's nice to have you with us," she added. "Many church members have called to leave you their good wishes. I'll type up their comments and e-mail them to you."

"Thanks, Darlene," Steven said. "I appreciate that you would do that, and I appreciate your willingness to stay and work for this ministry, even though things have changed."

When he'd hung up the phone, he turned his attention to other items on his desk. Bishop Johnson had handled his business well, so, at least Steven wasn't trying to dig himself out of a hole like he'd been forced to do when he'd become pastor of the church in St. Louis. Still, there was a lot to learn, and he almost wished that Bishop Johnson had decided to hang around for a few more weeks. But, with the help of Barbara Peters, Darlene Scott, and, Lord willing, Melinda, Steven was positive that things would soon begin to click for him.

He opened the folder Barbara Peters had put together to introduce him to the other pastors in their fellowship. It included a detailed biography of each pastor, the name of his church, and even a photo, to help Steven match names with faces.

At seventy-nine, Pastor David Lakes was the oldest and most experienced pastor in the fellowship. His photo showed a well-built man with a clean-shaven head. His son, Pastor Peter Lakes, was thirty-five and the youngest pastor in their fellowship. Pastor Joe Jackson wore a muscle shirt in the picture Barbara had provided. His ministry was in Memphis, Tennessee.

Steven could tell that Pastor Richard Bernard was handsome and a sharp dresser from his picture, but the info sheet about him also stated that, by the age of thirty-six, he had already been divorced twice. Bishop Johnson had received complaints about how friendly Pastor

Bernard was with the young female church members, and he had counseled him, but also threatened to have him removed from his church if any additional complaints surfaced. Steven hoped that Pastor Bernard had gotten his life back on track with God, because he would have no problem carrying out Bishop Johnson's warning.

Two other pastors in the fellowship had churches in Georgia—Leonard Martin's in Macon, James Woodson's in Alpharetta. With more than nine thousand members, James Woodson's church easily surpassed all the others in size.

Pastor Bo Prather was a flamboyant, fifty-year-old faith teacher from Dallas, Texas. Donald Toler was a pastor out of Toledo, Ohio, with a remarkable healing ministry. Matt Dineen was the only white pastor in the fellowship. His Houston, Texas, church was diverse and growing so fast that the congregation hadn't been able to worship in the same church building for more than five years before needing to move on to a bigger building.

Two other churches in the fellowship were also in Maryland, and Steven made a note to visit their pastors in the coming week. He hoped that he would have productive, long-lasting relationships with Pastors Nick Smalls and Ryan Thomas.

Reading over the information on the pastors within his fellowship, Steven recognized that most of these men could have taken over for Bishop Johnson. They had more than adequate qualifications. The realization caused Steven to think about Melinda all over again, and he faced the fact that she probably had been right. Bishop Johnson had definitely been acting with ulterior motives when he'd offered Steven his position. But Steven wasn't just some young stud. Bishop Johnson had promised Steven that his being chosen was about more than Melinda, and that he was confident Steven could do the job effectively.

Bishop Johnson had taken a chance on Steven, and Steven didn't want to let him down. He didn't care what Bishop Johnson's motives had been; he planned to work night and day, if he had to, in order to earn the respect of the other pastors in his fellowship and prove himself a faithful, godly bishop.

A knock on his door turned his attention away from the papers on his desk. "Come in," he said.

His door opened, and Melinda walked in. "Hey, Steven," she said, closing the door behind her. "I'm glad you asked to speak with me this morning. I owe you an apology, and I was going to ask Barbara to set up a meeting so that I could deliver it."

Steven leaned back in his seat. This he had to hear. "Did you just say that you owe me an apology?"

"Yes," Melinda said as she sat down in the chair in front of his desk. "I don't think that what my father did was right, but I shouldn't have taken my anger out on you—or anyone else in this congregation, for that matter. I've been praying about the situation, and I just wanted you to know that I'm going to try to conduct myself in a manner that would be pleasing to God from here on out."

"Thank you, Melinda. I'm glad you had a chance to pray about everything."

"Now, what did you want to see me about?"

Steven straightened his posture and opened the file labeled "Missions and Community Outreach." "I wanted to ask you a few questions about your upcoming mission trip," he said, handing Melinda a few of the papers from inside the file.

Melinda looked down at the papers for a moment and then back up at Steven. "What's your question?"

"For starters, I was wondering about the price tag of this trip. Twenty-five thousand dollars seems like an awful lot for two weeks."

Melinda nodded. "It would be, if the price covered only me. But I usually take along a few nurses, doctors, and missionaries on these trips. We also give anywhere from three to five thousand dollars for continued missions work in those areas."

"You're doing a great work, Melinda. And I wouldn't attempt to put a price tag on a soul that's saved or someone's body that's healed through proper medical attention."

Melinda leaned forward in her seat. "I hear a 'But...' in there somewhere."

Smiling, Steven continued, "Bishop Johnson showed me the proposal for the new Church Life Center—you've seen the blueprints, right? The building will be magnificent, and it should enable us to do so much to help the local community."

Melinda nodded. "I especially like the fact that we're going to build a few homes for the elderly."

"There's definitely enough room on the complex," Steven agreed, "so, why not build something for the very people who helped build this church?" He paused. "What do you think of the Family Life wing? We're going to offer all types of recreation for the kids."

Melinda didn't ever mince words, so she told Steven flat out, "I don't like the design of the Family Life wing. I think it covers all bases for young children and teens, but it doesn't have anything for their mothers and fathers. And who do you think will have to bring the kids to the Life Church in the first place?"

Steven tapped a finger on his chin as he thought about Melinda's comment. Finally, he said, "You make a good point. But what do you suggest we do for the parents?"

"Why not add a Fitness wing? It would give the parents something to do while waiting for their children—something that can lead to better health." When she finished her statement, Melinda lifted her hand. "Wait a minute," she said. "We've gotten off topic. What exactly is the problem you have with my upcoming mission trip?"

Steven hesitated for a moment. He and Melinda had been having a pleasant conversation, and he didn't want to ruin it. However, he had a job to do; Melinda would just have to understand that. "Actually, we are on the right subject. It is because of how expensive the building project will be that I must ask you to cut back on the trip expenses."

Melinda was silent for a moment, but when she finally spoke, her voice was calm and steady. "Just how do you suggest I cut back? The people I take with me are absolutely vital to the mission, and there's no getting around the costs of supplies."

Surprised that Melinda's tone didn't sound accusatory or angry, Steven leaned forward and engaged her further. "Well, I know that you plan two of these trips each year. Would you be willing to just do one for the next two years?"

"But we go to different places, and the needs are so great in the areas where we minister that I wouldn't want to cancel either of the trips."

"Okay," Steven said, pausing to think. "Would you be willing to put a team together that would help you raise half the money for the trip? We did things like that at my previous church."

Melinda lowered her head, looking contemplative, then looked back up at Steven. "We've never had to do that before, but I do agree that the building campaign is important, and that we need to rein in our spending in order to get that project moving."

"Thank you for being willing to compromise, Melinda."

"I can understand the wisdom in asking each ministry to tighten its belt. But I just want to make sure you understand how important our missions ministry is, and that you'll support it."

Steven raised his right hand. "You have my full support, Melinda. I believe in missions, and I wouldn't dare try to minimize your work. Just so you know, the other elders are being asked to cut back on expenses in some of their programs, too."

"I'm not an elder," Melinda reminded him, standing up.

"That's right. I didn't mean to imply—"

"Is there anything else I can help you with?"

It seemed to Steven that the room had suddenly become a bit chilly, and he wished that he hadn't misspoken and grouped Melinda with the church elders. But, based on the documents he'd just reviewed that detailed the elders' responsibilities, Melinda basically fit right in with them. He wasn't willing to start a conversation about that, though, so he turned to something else that was on his mind. "I also wanted to let you know that I had no idea Brianna was hiding out in your office this morning."

The apparent tension on Melinda's face gave way to a sincere-looking smile. "That daughter of yours is something else. I wasn't bothered at all by seeing her."

Steven stood up. "Well, I just didn't want you to think I told her to hug you and say that you felt like her mother."

"Relax, Steven. I'm not going to expect anything to develop between us because of anything my father has said, or because Brianna forms an attachment to me."

Laughing, Steven walked around his desk to stand closer to Melinda. "I didn't think that at all, Ms. Melinda Johnson. You're more than capable of strong-arming me into doing anything you want, if you choose to. Isn't that what you told me when we were eleven years old and you wanted a second helping of my mother's peach cobbler?"

Melinda shook her head, then turned to walk out of the office. "How can you possibly remember every little thing about our childhood?"

Steven opened the door for her, but he didn't answer her question. After Melinda left his office, he closed the door and stood with his back against it for a moment. Her question had caught him off guard. Now that he thought about it, he really did have a photographic memory of their childhood. Melinda was right. He still remembered so much about the times they'd spent together, probably because he'd rehearsed and rehashed the memories in the years following their breakup. Even during his marriage to Sylvia, Steven hadn't been able to get Melinda completely off his mind. But he knew that sweet memories wouldn't do him any good when Melinda was clearly not interested in returning to the way they had once been.

Heck, Steven couldn't say for sure that Melinda had been all that interested even when they'd been together. Almost all she'd ever talked about the last few years had been her call to the ministry and how much she wanted to do for the Lord. While Steven had found her hunger for God admirable, he'd decided he would need more from the woman who would be his wife. He'd tried to explain that to Melinda on numerous occasions, but she hadn't heard him; she'd only accused him of trying to take her dreams away. How would his life look now if he had given her dreams a chance?

eleven

AFTER COMPLETING HIS FAREWELL TOUR, BISHOP Johnson came back to Baltimore with some bad news. Pastor Richard Bernard, whose church was in Atlanta, had been diagnosed with colon cancer and needed to step down so that he could concentrate on healing.

Steven heard the news over dinner at Bishop Johnson's house while Melinda and Brianna were out shopping, and he immediately pushed his plate away, having lost his appetite. "I'm sorry to hear that. From your notes on Pastor Bernard, it seemed like he'd been getting his life back on track."

"I was sorry to hear it, too, because he really had been turning his life around," Bishop Johnson said, standing up. "Let's finish this conversation in my study."

When they sat down, Steven turned to Bishop Johnson and asked, "So, how do you want to handle this?"

The Bishop had this "My name is Bennett, and I ain't in it" look on his face. "Part of me wants to say that I'm retired, and that it isn't my problem. But I've walked through the fire with Pastor Bernard, so I know how far God has brought him. I think I owe him the courtesy of showing up during his time of need."

Steven rubbed his temples. "I've been bishop for only five weeks, and I had no idea I'd have to deal with something like this so soon. I appreciate your help on this one."

"Of course," said Bishop Johnson. "So, when do you want to go to Atlanta to help Pastor Bernard figure this out?"

At the thought of leaving town, Steven's mind drifted to Brianna. She'd been doing so much better since they'd relocated to Baltimore, but he wasn't sure if she could handle his leaving town so soon, even if it was for only a few days.

"Are you worried about Brianna?" Bishop Johnson asked, as if reading his mind.

Steven didn't want to seem like he wasn't willing to make personal sacrifices for the job Bishop Johnson had entrusted to him. So, rather than admitting that he was hesitant to travel outside of Baltimore, he tried playing it cool. "Why would you ask me that?"

Bishop Johnson chuckled. "You don't have to pretend, son. I know you don't want to leave Brianna. But, the fact is, you have an issue on your hands that needs to be resolved immediately."

"So, what are you saying? That we need to be out of here tomorrow?"

Bishop Johnson shrugged his shoulders. "If not tomorrow, then the day after, at the latest."

"Is it possible to wait until the weekend? I can't just pull Brianna out of school every time I need to leave town."

"The way I see it, you need either a wife or a nanny," Bishop Johnson said with a gleeful smirk on his face.

Ignoring his comment about a wife, Steven said, "Even if I had a nanny, I wouldn't leave Brianna with her to go out of town."

Rolling his eyes heavenward, Bishop Johnson said, "Pastor Bernard is scheduled to have surgery next week, and he wants to be able to tell his congregation who their new pastor will be before he leaves. Why don't you let go of your pride and ask Melinda to watch Brianna so that we can go and settle this matter?"

Raising his hands in surrender, Steven said, "Hey, it's not me. Melinda doesn't like me." He pointed at Bishop Johnson. "She doesn't like you much, either."

Bishop Johnson stood up and walked over to the window. Gazing out, he asked, "Do you think she'll ever get over what I did?"

"I don't know, sir. Melinda is pretty headstrong. And I'm not sure you truly understood what Melinda wants out of life."

"I know what she wants," Bishop Johnson said as he turned back to Steven. "And you should be the last one to talk, my friend. You refused to marry Melinda unless she gave up her dream of becoming a preacher."

True, Steven had done that. But, today, he wasn't exactly proud of himself for having passed up marriage to Melinda just because he hadn't wanted to be wed to a woman preacher. As he'd been working with Melinda over the past few weeks, he'd seen the sheer joy she got from serving the Lord, and it sickened him to think of what they could have done by serving together as husband and wife. Even though he still opposed her becoming a pastor, it was clear to Steven that Melinda was a woman after God's heart. "Can I ask you something, sir?"

Bishop Johnson nodded as he sat back down.

"Why didn't you ever appoint Melinda as an elder in our church? She seems more qualified for the position than some of the men you did appoint."

For a moment, there was silence in the room. Bishop Johnson steepled his hands under his chin and got a pensive look on his face. Finally, he said, "I considered making Melinda an elder. But, for so many years, I thought that she would become pastor of the church once I retired that I just never bothered to appoint her to that position."

"But you didn't appoint her as pastor. You gave that job to me, and now, Melinda doesn't like me." Steven paused. "Well, she treats me kindly and seems...tolerant. Still, the friendship we once had is gone."

"Well, you could always right my wrong," said Bishop Johnson. "I'm praying that Pastor Bernard will be back in the pulpit within a few months. But, in the interim, why don't you consider giving the pastoral position at his church to Melinda?"

"And go completely against my convictions regarding female pastors?" Steven asked, without missing a beat.

"They've got plenty of preaching women in Atlanta," Bishop Johnson said. "No one will think you're doing something controversial or contrary to your beliefs. Plus, maybe Melinda will find a husband down there."

Steven stood up and began to pace up and down, trying to get a handle on how he felt about the idea. The thought of Melinda living so far away was troubling; although their relationship was rocky, he still had hopes of total reconciliation. And, to tell the truth, the notion of Melinda finding someone in Atlanta to marry didn't set so well with him, either. But he wasn't about to admit any of that to Bishop Johnson. "Melinda is doing such a good job in her ministry," he said. "Plus, I don't think she's ready to become a pastor."

"She's not ready, or you're not ready?" Bishop Johnson countered.

"With all due respect, sir, you gave me this job knowing full well my opinion on women preachers. It hasn't changed. And I'm not one to act against my beliefs, even if it's for a temporary fix."

Just then, they heard the front door open. Bishop Johnson looked like he was about to say something, but he stood up and walked out to the entryway to greet Melinda and Brianna. Steven followed him out and watched the two drop their armfuls of shopping bags on the floor.

"Hey, you two," Bishop Johnson said, giving Melinda a kiss, while Steven hugged Brianna. "Did you leave anything for the other customers?" he added with a laugh.

Brianna giggled, and Melinda said, "We tried hard not to, but a credit card can go only so far."

Brianna turned to Steven. "Daddy, wait till I show you the outfits Melinda bought for me. I just love them."

"You can show me when we get home, sweetie," Steven told her. Then, turning to Melinda, he asked, "How much do I owe you?"

Melinda waved off his question. "Just about everything we purchased was on sale. It didn't cost that much. And, besides," she said, winking at Brianna, "I can't charge for a girls' day out."

Bishop Johnson yawned. "Well, Steven, I'm going to go upstairs to pack for our trip."

"Daddy, don't tell me you're leaving again. You just got home last night!" Melinda said.

Bishop Johnson patted his daughter on the back. "Steven and I need to take care of some business in Atlanta."

Melinda eyed her father suspiciously, then asked, "What's going on in Atlanta?"

"I'll tell you about it later," he said, then turned to head upstairs. "See you in the morning, Steven," he said over his shoulder.

Brianna turned to Steven. "We're going out of town?" she asked.

Steven lowered himself on one knee, looked into his little girl's eyes, and prayed silently that she wouldn't have another panic attack at the mention of his leaving her. He took a deep breath, bracing himself for an outburst of tears. "Bishop Johnson and I have to make a quick trip to Atlanta. But you can't go with me on this trip, honey. We have to leave tomorrow, and you have school."

Brianna's bottom lip began to quiver. "You're leaving me?"

"Only for a day or two. I promise I won't be gone long," Steven said, his heart breaking to see the fear in his daughter's eyes.

But then, Brianna totally surprised him. She turned her sad eyes in Melinda's direction and asked, "Are you going with them, Ms. Melinda?"

Melinda smiled kindly and shook her head. "No, sweetie. I'm not going out of town."

"Then, can I stay with you while Daddy is away?"

Steven gave Melinda an apologetic look, then turned back to Brianna. "I was going to call Grandma to see if you could spend a few days with her and Grandpa."

"But I want to stay with Melinda," Brianna whimpered.

Melinda crouched down next to Steven and squeezed Brianna's arm. "You know what, Brianna? I think I would like some company in this big, old house. If it's okay with your dad, why don't you go home, pack some clothes, and come back here first thing in the morning?"

Brianna's eyes brightened. "You mean it? I can stay with you?"

"Of course, you can."

"Oh, please, Daddy? May I stay with Ms. Melinda?" Brianna pleaded.

Steven looked to Melinda with questioning eyes, and she nodded a confirmation. "Well, okay—if you promise to be on your best behavior."

Brianna squealed with delight and hugged Melinda.

Steven had grown up with Melinda and come close to marrying her before the whole thing had blown up in their faces. Since then, he had never thought he'd want Melinda to be a part of his life again. But, here he was, watching his daughter hug his ex-fiancée. Suddenly, Steven didn't want Melinda to be his ex-anything.

Sitting in the middle of her bed with piles of papers all around her, Melinda said a quick prayer for sanity. She would be babysitting Brianna for the next two days and probably wouldn't have time to work on her fund-raising campaign for the mission trip to Uganda. In the past five weeks, Melinda had put together a committee with the sole responsibility of raising funds. Among other strategies, the group had been passing out flyers to the members of Omega to promote the giving campaign. So far, though, the church members hadn't quite caught on to the giving part. In two weeks' time, they'd received only two hundred dollars in donations. That was a long way from the ten thousand they'd need before the team left for Uganda.

Melinda considered the other fund-raising events they'd been planning, including a car wash and a fashion show. At this point, she gladly would even sell chicken dinners, a practice her father frowned on. He'd always said that if the church didn't take in enough tithe money to pay for the things they were planning to do, then perhaps they shouldn't do them.

As if he knew she was thinking about him, Bishop Johnson knocked on her door and then poked his head into her room. "Are you busy?"

Melinda gathered a few of the papers that covered her bed. "Just trying to deal with my money crunch issues."

"Do you want me to come back later?" he asked.

"No, no. Come on in." She plopped the papers back on the bed. "I'm tired of worrying about how we're going to raise this money, anyway."

Bishop Johnson took a seat in the overstuffed chair next to Melinda's bed. "Steven told me that he's asked everyone to cut back and find ways to earn some of the money for programs. I can't say I would have done it that way, but he is right about one thing—we have been spending more than we've been bringing in over the past few years. And there's no way we can continue operating like that."

Melinda swung her legs over the side of her bed and balanced on the edge. "Dad, you never told me that the church was having financial problems."

"We're not, really. We have so much saved that we've been able to cover the shortfall that's occurred in the last few years. Our programs just kept growing while the economic situation of our members got worse during the recent recession. And, don't forget, we still need to raise enough funds to build the new Church Life Center. So, I think it's good that Steven is making some changes."

"If I had known, I would have suggested the same thing to you. There's no way to run a church by spending more than what comes in." Melinda looked away from her father as she added, "But you didn't give me the chance."

Bishop Johnson put his hand on Melinda's knee. Creases lined his brow, and his eyes looked shaded in sadness. "It seems like my decision to hire Steven has put a wedge between us, and I want to remove it."

Melinda sighed. "I guess I just don't understand why you did this. I always thought I could trust you, of all people, to keep your promises, but I don't know anymore."

She stood up and walked over to the window on the opposite side of the room, then peered out at the rose garden she'd planted in the backyard below. Seeing the colorful flowers and the intricate rock work surrounding them usually brought her peace—something she'd known little of since her father had denied her the fulfillment of a lifelong dream.

"I didn't do this to hurt you, Melinda."

"No, you did it to help me get a husband." She turned away from the window and stood before her father. "Did you think that depriving me of the pastoral position would make me so desperate that I'd marry the pastor just to get close to the pulpit?"

"Honey, why are you still so angry with Steven over something that happened ten years ago? Breaking off the engagement was your idea, as I understand it, and you told me that you'd forgiven him."

Melinda had never told her father that she and Steven had slept together the night before they'd left for college. For years, she'd thought that God would never forgive her for what she'd done. When her father had promised her the pastoral position upon his retirement, Melinda had felt that God had finally forgiven her. But, then, Steven had voiced his disapproval, demanding that she give up her God-given calling. Melinda had determined not to allow Steven to take the one thing that she considered proof of God's forgiveness. And, now, she was obligated to go up against her father for the right to do what God had called her to do—the mission God had given back to her, even after she'd sinned. "It's not about Steven, Daddy. You went back on your word, and I just don't know how to trust you anymore. If a woman comes along who's been anointed by God to pastor, men like you and Steven shut the door in her face and tell her to go, get married, and have children."

Bishop Johnson lowered his head, then looked up again with tears in his eyes. "I'm sorry, baby girl. I thought I was doing the right thing. I don't know if this will make it up to you, but Richard Bernard is ill, and he wants to step down so that he can concentrate on recovering."

Shocked, Melinda let her jaw hang slack for a moment. She sat back down on the edge of her bed. "What's wrong with him?"

"He has cancer."

"I'm sorry to hear that. I know I've never thought much of Pastor Bernard, but I wouldn't have wished something like that on him."

"I know you wouldn't have. But the thing I wanted to talk to you about is your stepping in for Pastor Bernard while he's out. This would be an interim position, because I truly believe that God is going to heal him. So, what do you think? Would you be willing to pastor Bernard's church for a season?"

"Of course, I would!" Melinda jumped up and hugged her father. Almost as quickly, she sat back down and frowned. "Wait a minute. You don't have control over pastoral appointments anymore. Those decisions are up to Steven now."

"Let me talk to Steven," her father said. "I'll work it out for you."

Melinda folded her arms across her chest. "What happened to your hopes of having a grandchild? Are you saying that you'd rather let me preach than push me to marry Steven?"

"I was wrong—I can see that now," Bishop Johnson said with a sigh. "I'm sorry, Melinda. I should have thought about what God was calling you to do, not what I decided was best for you."

With an understanding smile, Melinda told her father, "I accept your apology. But, I don't want you to talk to Steven. If you're truly sorry and want to make it up to me, let me handle this myself."

twelve

MELINDA AND BRIANNA WERE IN THE LIVING ROOM watching the Disney classic *Beauty and the Beast* when Brianna suddenly turned to Melinda and hugged her so tightly that Melinda thought she might pass out. "What was that for, sweetie?" Melinda asked when Brianna released her.

"I'm just glad I'm here with you," Brianna responded. She laid her head on Melinda's shoulder and continued watching the movie.

Melinda had intended to play the movie for Brianna so that she could get caught up on paperwork before Steven returned. She was planning to ask for the Atlanta interim pastoral position, but she didn't want to leave anything undone with her current position. Instead, she'd left the paperwork untouched for more than an hour while watching the movie with Brianna. She'd promised herself that she would do some work later that evening, but now, she heard herself asking Brianna, "Would you like to bake some cookies?"

Brianna lifted her head off Melinda's shoulder, and her eyes lit up. "What kind?"

"Hmm…I think I have the ingredients we'd need for either peanut butter or oatmeal cookies."

With a mischievous grin on her face, Brianna asked, "Can we do both?"

"You mean, peanut butter oatmeal cookies?"

Brianna nodded eagerly.

"You got it," Melinda said, jumping up from the couch. "I'll go get everything ready in the kitchen if you want to stay here and finish the movie."

Brianna picked up the remote control and pressed Stop. "I've seen *Beauty and the Beast* at least nine hundred and ninety-nine times. I'll help you in the kitchen."

Melinda laughed at Brianna's outrageous claim. "Well, then, I must apologize for making you suffer through the movie for the thousandth time."

"That's all right. I enjoyed watching it with you. We can watch another old movie after we make the cookies, if you want," Brianna said.

Melinda laughed even harder. Children were such a kick. They said exactly what they thought without worrying about how it sounded. She grabbed a bag of flour and a sack of sugar out of the pantry, then pulled out a jar of peanut butter and a canister of oats. "Can you find eggs, milk, and butter in the fridge?" she asked Brianna.

"Okay," Brianna said, trotting over to the refrigerator and opening the door.

Melinda opened a cabinet and took out a couple of mixing bowls, setting them on the table so that Brianna would be able to reach them easily. She helped Brianna measure out the ingredients, then handed her a spoon for stirring.

"How does this look?" Brianna asked when she had mixed the oats, flour, and sugar with the eggs, milk, butter, and peanut butter.

Melinda inspected the contents of the bowl. "It looks perfect, but I forgot the baking soda and cinnamon," she said, opening the cabinet again.

"Cinnamon?" Brianna said. "What do we need that for?"

Melinda licked her lips and then smacked them together as if tasting something scrumptious. "Cinnamon makes everything taste better."

"Everything?" Brianna asked with a skeptical tone.

"Okay, maybe not everything. But cinnamon does make a lot of things taste so much better, like pancakes, peach cobbler, and definitely oatmeal cookies." Melinda opened the container of cinnamon and sprinkled a generous amount into the dough for Brianna to mix in.

Melinda sprayed the baking sheets with cooking spray, and she and Brianna scooped spoonfuls of cookie dough onto them, tasting an occasional sample, of course.

When the baking sheets were in the oven, they settled on the couch with mugs of steaming tea and waited for the cookies to bake. Out of the blue, Brianna turned to Melinda and said, "Why don't you like my daddy?"

Melinda almost choked on a sip of tea. She sat up straight and set her mug on the coffee table. "Excuse me?"

"My daddy, Ms. Melinda. I know you don't like him. But, I was thinking that if you did, we could bake cookies together all the time."

"Brianna, it's not true that I don't like your dad. We just have some...different opinions. But what does my liking or not liking him have to do with our baking cookies?"

With the wisdom of a seven-year-old, Brianna said, "Well, the way I see it, if you liked my daddy, the two of you could get married, and then you and I could bake cookies and watch movies and do all sorts of fun things together all the time."

Little does she know how close we came to marriage before, Melinda thought, realizing that Brianna would not be with her right now, had she and Steven gone through with it. She decided to try changing the subject. "Okay,

so, you've seen *Beauty and the Beast* a thousand times...
what other old Disney movies have you seen?"

Fortunately, Brianna took the bait without protest.
"I've seen *The Little Mermaid.*"

"What about *Cinderella*?"

"Nope."

"*Snow White and the Seven Dwarfs?*"

"Haven't seen that one, either. I have some books
about Cinderella and Snow White, but I don't have those
movies."

"You've missed out, girl. We're going to have to do
something about that," Melinda said, standing. "I'm going
to check on the cookies. I'll be right back."

Brianna jumped up and grabbed Melinda's hand. "I'll
help you, I *like* helping you." As they walked hand in hand
to the kitchen, Brianna added, "If you liked my daddy, I
could help you with a lot of things."

Melinda wanted to tell Brianna that she had liked her
daddy once upon a time—he'd been her Prince Charm-
ing—and he'd broken her heart. But she didn't think that
such a detail was appropriate to share with an innocent
seven-year-old who was just looking for a replacement
mommy. She stopped in her tracks, bent down, and gave
Brianna a big hug. "I wish I could do more things with
you, too, Brianna."

Most of the churches in the fellowship held a Bible
study on Wednesday nights, but Pastor Richard Bernard
held his on Tuesdays. When Steven and Bishop Johnson
walked into the sanctuary, Pastor Bernard was already
behind the pulpit, preaching a message of grace. Steven
sat down and listened as he told his congregation that
they shouldn't condemn themselves for their sins. He

emphasized that God was a forgiving God, and that grace was one of the best things He had come up with.

Pastor Bernard asked the congregation to turn to Psalm 84:11, and then he read aloud, *"The Lord God is a sun and shield; the Lord will give grace and glory; no good thing will He withhold from those who walk uprightly."*

That was one of Steven's favorite Scriptures. As he continued to listen, he found himself spiritually stretched by the sermon.

Looking around the sanctuary, Steven could tell that many of the people were truly engaged by the message. Pastor Bernard could whoop, holler, and preach—that was for sure. Thinking of the pastor's past issues, Steven reminded himself that church leaders weren't superhuman beings. No matter his eloquence or spiritual wisdom, a pastor could fall just as easily as another man.

When the sermon was finished, Pastor Bernard looked directly at Steven and Bishop Johnson. "We have some special guests with us tonight," he announced. "Will the two gentlemen from Baltimore please stand up?"

Steven glanced over at Bishop Johnson, and the two of them rose from their seats.

"You all know Bishop Langston Johnson, who recently retired. He was here not too long ago on his farewell tour of the fellowship," Pastor Bernard explained. "The man standing next to him is our new bishop, Steven Marks, formerly of St. Louis. On your way out tonight, please act like y'all have manners and greet Bishop Marks and Bishop Johnson."

The two bishops smiled and waved at the congregation and then sat back down so that Pastor Bernard could conclude the service and pronounce the benediction.

As they made their ways to Pastor Bernard's office after the service, Steven and Bishop Johnson received warm welcomes from many church members. Once inside his office, the two men sat down on the couch, while Pastor Bernard reclined in the La-Z-Boy next to the couch. "Thank you both for coming down here so quickly," he said.

Steven had enjoyed Bernard's sermon, and the humble expression on the man's face made Steven feel at ease in his presence. He wanted to get to know this man who had fallen and was now not only in the process of fighting his way back to God, but also fighting a deadly disease. "I wish we could have visited for a different reason," he said.

"Me, too," Pastor Bernard agreed.

"From that message you just preached, I can tell that you're ready to fight," Bishop Johnson said. "And we're going to be in this fight with you, Richard. We're going to fight with our faith, and I truly believe that God is going to bring you through this."

"Amen, Bishop. From your mouth to God's ears. I'm only forty-nine, so I'm not interested in checking out of here anytime soon. But, I have to tell you, something like this really makes you understand how important family is." Pastor Bernard took a deep breath and then said, "Both of you lost your wives while your children were young. So, I'm sure you understand what I'm talking about. I don't want my wife to be left alone to raise our two youngest children."

"I understand exactly what you're talking about," Steven said. "Trying to get my daughter Brianna through the death of her mother has been one of the most difficult things I have ever had to do."

Bishop Johnson cleared his throat. "Look, Richard. I'm sure you want to get home, so we're not going to take

114 • Vanessa Miller

up too much of your time tonight. We'll be back in the morning to go over the details of your proposal, but what I don't understand is why you want us to remove you from your post."

"Well, Bishop, I really feel like my church has been through enough with me. I haven't always done the right thing, as you know. I don't want to hurt the church by leaving the congregation in a state of uncertainty as to whether they have a pastor."

"I understand what you're saying, Pastor Bernard. But, if you want to come back after you recover, we'd rather it be made known that the person taking your place would be doing it for only a season," Steven said.

"It means a lot to me that you would want me back. I truly do want to continue preaching. I'm just hoping God has the same idea."

"Of course, we'll want you back," Steven assured him. "Bishop Johnson has told me about your struggles, but he's also talked about how much you have strived to do the right thing in recent years."

Bishop Johnson spoke up. "Before we go any further, let's pray for Pastor Bernard. I'm discerning feelings of fear. Before we can install someone in your place, Richard—even if only temporarily—you have to believe that you are going to survive this ordeal." He stood up and reached out to take Steven and Pastor Bernard's hands. As they stood, too, he began, "Lord, we come to You now, lifting our brother, Richard Bernard, up to You. Your Word says it is by Your stripes that we are healed...."

As Bishop Johnson was praying, Pastor Bernard fell to his knees and cried out to God to heal him. When they'd said "Amen," Bernard stood up again, looking alert and refreshed. "Okay, Bishop. I'm a believer. I will survive.

And, since that is the case, I think we need to make sure to inform the interim pastor that I'll be coming back."

"I like the way you're talking. Sounds a lot like faith," Bishop Johnson said.

"One person in our fellowship comes to mind whom I think would accept the pastoral position, knowing that it wasn't for keeps, and that's your daughter, Melinda," Pastor Bernard said to Bishop Johnson. "How about it? Do you think she'd be willing to come down here and help me out?"

Steven didn't like that kind of talk. He turned to Bishop Johnson and said, "We should probably let Pastor Bernard get home to his family and finish this conversation in the morning."

"That's a good idea," Bishop Johnson said. He turned to Pastor Bernard. "Go home and get yourself some rest, and we'll figure all this out in the morning."

Pastor Bernard thanked them and saw them to the door.

⸻

As they got into the rental car in the parking lot, Bishop Johnson said, "Let's get something to eat before we check into our hotel."

Steven agreed, and he drove along until they reached the town of Buckhead, the local home of Bishop Johnson's favorite restaurant, the Cheesecake Factory. When they'd been seated and had placed their orders, Steven said, "I've been thinking about this interim pastor position. I read through all the files that Barbara put together for me on the pastors of the other churches in our fellowship, and I noticed that you had, at one point, considered one of the elders at Pastor Bernard's church for a pastoral position. Do you think he might be good for the interim role?"

Bishop Johnson waited to answer as their server refilled their glasses of iced tea. He took a sip, then said, "I assume you're referring to Joel Lewis. He is an anointed man with a heart for the people, but I was looking for someone who also has a strong, outgoing personality to pastor that church."

When the server returned with their meals, the men said grace before digging in. Savoring his salmon with rice, Bishop Johnson mulled over his promise to Melinda that he wouldn't butt in. He had intended to honor her wishes; however, Bernard had already thrown her name into the mix, so he didn't see any harm in adding his two cents. He swallowed a bite of salmon and said, "You could just go with Bernard's suggestion and let Melinda handle his church for a time."

Steven had just taken a bite of his chicken burrito, so he chewed quickly and then swallowed before sputtering, "B-b-but—" He closed his mouth, took a deep breath, and then tried again. "I thought you wanted Melinda to work with me."

"I made a mistake. She's not happy." He hoped Steven would see the wisdom in his proposal.

"We've been working together for only five weeks," Steven replied. "Melinda will soon get used to the new reality."

Bishop Johnson put his fork down and stared at him. "I thought you would be thrilled at the chance to get Melinda out of your way. The only thing that could be holding you back is this problem you have with women preaching. And I have to tell you, Steven, I simply don't agree with it."

Steven took a moment to think about Bishop Johnson's statement. Growing up, he hadn't known any women who considered themselves preachers. His father had said that a woman's place was in the home, waiting on her man, hand and foot. Consequently, Steven had married a woman who had been more than willing to be a stay-at-home mom. Although he'd loved Sylvia with all of his heart, he'd never felt the same kind of deep connection with her that he'd had with Melinda. He and Melinda had spoken the same language, shared the same dreams—except for Melinda's dream of preaching, that is.

In the last ten years, Steven had watched women like Anne Graham Lotz and Joyce Meyer evangelize the nation while keeping their marriages intact. He'd met and admired Yvonne Milner, who copastored a church in Detroit with her husband of more than thirty years. Steven had met still other women who were dedicated to the cause of Christ's kingdom. At times, Steven had wanted to applaud them, but he'd always felt this gnawing sense in the back of his mind that something about what they were doing was not in line with God's original plan.

He looked at Bishop Johnson and answered honestly, "My dad always told me that women shouldn't preach. He referred to 1 Timothy 2:11–14 so many times when I was growing up that it became imbedded in my ways of thinking."

"Well, I guess I can't fault you for your honesty. But I'm calling in a favor on this one. It's only an interim position, and I want Melinda to have it."

Bishop Johnson's constant push for him to send Melinda to Atlanta made Steven examine his feelings. He knew that he didn't want Melinda to be hundreds of miles away from him anymore. He needed her close to him and close to Brianna; she'd been the force that had been keeping a smile on his daughter's face—and on his face, too—for the past few weeks. And, truth be told, he didn't want that to end.

Steven picked up his napkin, wiped his mouth, and then pushed his plate aside. "I have to be honest with you, sir. Some of my motives for not wanting Melinda to take this position are selfish. Recently, I've been thinking about what she suggested you had in mind when I first arrived."

Bishop Johnson had a blank look on his face, so Steven continued, "You said that a bishop needs a wife, and that Melinda and I would be good for each other. I've been wondering if that might not be true."

Bishop Johnson's deadpan face showed sudden astonishment, followed by a broad smile. "Forgive me if I seem a bit speechless, but, didn't you tell me that you weren't interested in Melinda at all?"

Steven propped his head on his hand and thought for a few seconds. When he lifted his gaze, he tried not to show the inner torture he felt. "I've always loved Melinda. My mother used to tell me that Melinda and I had fallen in love as babies. I don't know if that is true or not, but I've never been able to forget her. I tried to put her out of my mind while I was married, because I knew I could never have her. But now...."

Bishop Johnson looked like he was about to jump out of his seat. "You know how I feel about it. I still want the two of you to get married." He leaned in closer. "Have you told Melinda how you feel?"

Steven shook his head. "I wanted to make sure that what I was feeling was true."

"Don't wait too long. I think she's getting antsy."

As fate would have it, Steven would not wait even another day. For, by the time he and Bishop Johnson had made it back to Pastor Bernard's office the next morning, Pastor Bernard had already called Melinda and told her that he'd recommended her for the position.

thirteen

"WHAT ARE YOU GETTING ALL DRESSED UP FOR?" Brianna asked Melinda as she walked into her bedroom.

Taking the rollers out of her hair, Melinda said, "Our fathers are on their way home from Atlanta. And, it seems that I've been invited to go out to dinner with the Bishop."

Picking up a silver bracelet from Melinda's vanity, Brianna said, "My mother had a bracelet just like this. I used to wear it all the time."

"Would you like to wear my bracelet, Brianna?" Melinda asked.

"Oh, can I? Can I, please?"

Melinda nodded as she put the bracelet around Brianna's wrist and fastened the clasp. Then, she smiled to see Brianna dance happily around the room, holding her arm out and watching the silver bracelet sparkle. Being with Brianna made Melinda wish that she had children of her own—especially ones as sweet as Brianna.

The little girl danced over to Melinda and rested her head on Melinda's arm. "Thank you for letting me wear this." She touched the bracelet and said, "I don't remember much about my mother anymore, but I do remember her bracelet." Lifting her head, she asked Melinda, "What do you remember most about your mother?"

Melinda had never liked talking about her mother. After she'd died, Melinda had tried to forget most of the memories of her, especially the one thing she'd done that had hurt Melinda the most. She didn't want to make anything up, so, she answered truthfully, "The thing I remember most is a promise my mother made to me and didn't keep. She promised me that she wouldn't die—but then she did, anyway. Even though everybody dies, and it was impossible for her to keep that promise, I was still very hurt. After that, I never wanted anyone to make me promises they couldn't keep." Melinda turned away from Brianna and resumed taking out her rollers. "That's enough chitchat for now—I need to finish getting ready!"

"Can I come along?"

"Not this time, honey. My dad and I have some things to discuss, which is probably why he's taking me out."

"Okay," Brianna said, taking the bracelet off her wrist and setting it back on Melinda's vanity before skipping out of the room.

As Melinda turned to watch Brianna leave, she was struck by the girl's remarkable attitude. Most children would have kept asking and then resorted to begging to get what they'd wanted, but not Brianna. She'd simply skipped out of the room as if she'd been offered the key to the city.

Melinda wished that she could have Brianna's attitude. She hadn't handled her recent disappointments well at all, she knew, but she was thankful that God still loved her and was working on her, day by day. Melinda had a good feeling about this dinner with her father. When Pastor Bernard had called her early that morning and told her that he had recommended her for the position of interim pastor, Melinda had appreciated the gesture, but she hadn't been sure if much would come of it, especially if Steven would have the final say. But when her father had called that afternoon and invited her to "dinner with the Bishop," she had thought, *This is it. Why else would we go out, if not to celebrate my becoming the interim pastor of the church in Atlanta?*

She finished combing out the curls in her hair and then stood up and admired her image in the full-length mirror on the wall opposite her vanity. Her father had suggested she wear the dress he'd bought her for Christmas. It was sleeveless, with a deep, chocolate color that complemented her skin tone. Form-fitting, it had an asymmetrical hemline and a satin tie across the waistline. Not to sound cocky, but she knew she looked good.

She had two different shoes on her feet, trying to decide which one looked better, when she heard Brianna yell, "They're here! They're here!" Seconds later, she burst into Melinda's room. "They're here, Ms. Melinda!"

Melinda laughed. "Go ahead and greet them. Tell them I'll be right down."

"Okay," Brianna said as she turned around, then raced out of Melinda's room and down the stairs.

Melinda was tempted to make them wait while she tried two other pairs of shoes, but her father's words resounded in her head: *"Never keep a man waiting, especially when he has the power to change your life."* So, she stuck with her brown, high-heeled sandals with the ankle laces, looked in the mirror one last time, and gave herself a pep talk. "This is it, Melinda. What God has planned for you is for you—don't ever forget that." Grabbing her purse from her bed, she turned off the light and walked out of her room, excited about the prospect of beginning to fulfill her destiny in Atlanta.

Steven was standing at the bottom of the stairs when Melinda started making her way down, and he was caught off guard by her beauty. She looked stunning in that sleeve-less dress, and he wanted to run up those stairs, pick her up, and carry her the rest of the way down. But he had to keep his cool, and so he stood there and acted as if the gorgeous woman coming toward him was just an ordinary lady, not someone he'd loved for the better part of a lifetime.

"Steven," Melinda said as she reached the bottom of the stairs. "How was your time in Atlanta?"

His mouth was glued shut—at least, that's the way it felt. He wanted to tell Melinda just how gorgeous she looked, but all he could do was stare at her. Just then, Brianna ran into the foyer and saved him from further humiliation.

"Doesn't Ms. Melinda look beautiful, Daddy?" Brianna asked, grabbing his hand.

"Out of the mouth of babes...." "Yes, she does. I was just thinking that."

"Okay, you two. No need to butter me up," Melinda said with a laugh. "I've already done my babysitting job."

"I don't think they're buttering you up, honey," came her father's voice. He strode into the foyer and said, "You're the most beautiful girl this side of heaven."

Why couldn't I have said something like that? Steven thought, silently chastising himself for merely cosigning Bri-anna's remark instead of coming up with an original com-pliment, like Bishop Johnson had. *Way to go, bonehead. You really know how to sweep a woman off her feet.*

Melinda gave her father a kiss. "Welcome home, Dad-dy. Now, stop embarrassing me."

Bishop Johnson smiled and gave Steven a pat on the back. "You two have a lot to discuss, so you should prob-ably get going. Brianna and I will be fine."

"But—I thought—wasn't this supposed to be a father-daughter dinner?" Melinda asked, sending her father a quizzical look.

Bishop Johnson was smiling like the cat that swallowed the canary. "I said it would be a dinner with the Bishop—and I meant Bishop Marks."

Melinda looked over at Steven, who smiled sheepishly and shrugged. "We figured a little omission would be necessary to get you to accept the invitation," he said.

Giving her shoulders a shrug of resignation, Melinda turned to her father. "Well, whatever you do, Daddy, don't make her watch *Beauty and the Beast*. She's already seen that 'old' movie a thousand times."

Brianna laughed. "I do like the movie. It's just that I know all the words, and I'm never surprised by what happens," she said.

Grinning, Bishop Johnson said, "I promise not to torture you like Melinda obviously did while your father and I were away."

Brianna shook her head fervently. "Oh, no. Ms. Melinda didn't torture me. I love spending time with her." She gave Melinda a hug, then looked up at her and asked, "You like spending time with me, too, don't you?"

"Of course, I do, Brianna. You're like the little sister I never had."

Scrunching up her nose, Brianna said, "You're too old to be my sister."

Melinda pretended to pinch Brianna's arm. "There you go again with those 'old' cracks. I'll have you know, Ms. Brianna Marks, that I am young in spirit."

"Yeah, me too," Steven chimed in. "These aches and pains I've been feeling recently don't mean a thing. I'm as young as I want to be."

Bishop Johnson cut short the conversation. "Okay, well, you two youngsters get on out of here so that Brianna and I can order a pizza and relax." Then, taking

Brianna's hand, he walked into the family room and left Steven and Melinda alone in the foyer.

"Well, uh, shall we?" Steven asked, holding open the front door and motioning for Melinda to go through. "After you."

On their way to the car, Melinda asked, "Where are we going?"

"I was thinking of going to the Inner Harbor…to McCormick & Schmick's," Steven almost mumbled.

Melinda turned and gave him a look that sent chills down his spine. "You didn't have to choose such an upscale restaurant," she said.

"Hey, I thought you would give me extra points for remembering how much you like the place," Steven replied, opening the passenger side door for Melinda.

Melinda shook her head as she ducked into the car. "I'm not keeping score tonight, Steven. Just drive."

On their way to Baltimore's Inner Harbor, Steven chastised himself yet again for being a bonehead—he had proposed to Melinda at McCormick & Schmick's; of course, she wouldn't want to go to that restaurant with him! He patted his pocket, hoping that the ring he'd purchased for her before he and Bishop Johnson had left Atlanta was still there. The way things had been going for him so far, he wouldn't have been surprised if he had left the ring in his suitcase. Thankfully, it was still in his jacket pocket.

When they arrived at the restaurant on Pier 5, Steven pulled up to the curb, handed his keys to the valet, and came around to open Melinda's door. As they walked up the stairs toward the restaurant entrance, they suddenly heard someone yell, "Lady J! Lady J!"

Melinda turned around. "That's Billy!" she exclaimed, then hurried back down the stairs, looking left and right.

Steven ambled down the stairs after her as the nearly sev-en-foot Billy Woods ran over and picked her up in a hug before quickly putting her back down.

"I made the team, Lady J!" Billy said excitedly. "I'm gonna be a true Terrapin. And I have a scholarship to cover half my tuition."

"That's awesome, Billy! Congratulations!" Melinda said, as Steven came up and stood behind her, trying not to look impatient.

The three were joined by a weary-looking woman who was almost two feet shorter than Billy. "Brenda, so good to see you!" Melinda said, wrapping her in a warm embrace. "You must be so proud of Billy."

"I couldn't believe it," Billy's mother said with a smile. "Nobody in my family has ever gone to college, let alone played college basketball. My boy's going to be somebody. And we have you to thank for that."

Melinda shook her head. "I'm not the one you need to thank. Everything I do is because the Lord Jesus gives me the strength to do it. So, if you're looking for someone to thank, look up."

Steven gently tapped Melinda's arm. "We'd better get in there before we give up our table," he said.

"Oh, that's right," she said to Steven, then turned back to Billy and his mother. "What are you two doing in the Inner Harbor tonight?"

"You know that restaurant in Little Italy, Amicci's? We're going there for a celebration dinner," Billy said, beaming from ear to ear.

"That sounds fun—maybe we could celebrate together!" Melinda said, then turned to Steven. "Could we have dinner at Amicci's, instead?"

Steven raised his hand to wave off her suggestion. "Sorry, but it's tough to get reservations here, and I'd hate to forfeit our table." Then, to Billy and his mother, he said, "We'll see you both later, though."

Ignoring the exasperated look on Melinda's face, he put an arm across her back and steered her toward the restaurant. He hoped that he hadn't ruined his plan to propose by stopping Melinda from ruining it....

When they were seated, Melinda leaned over the table and said in a quiet yet stern voice, "That was rude, Steven. Why weren't you willing to change our plans so that we could celebrate with Billy and his mother?"

"I wasn't trying to be rude. I just wanted to talk to you in private, that's all."

"You act as if you're jealous of Billy or something. It just doesn't make any sense the way you treat him is wrong. You didn't even congratulate him."

"Sorry. You're right, I should have done that. I'll be sure to congratulate him the next time I see him. I guess I had something else on my mind."

Silence prevailed for a full five minutes as they studied their menus. When the server came to take their orders, Melinda ordered the wild Alaskan halibut, while Steven ordered a surf-and-turf dish of filet mignon and jumbo stuffed shrimp. Alone again, they sat in silence until Steven finally spoke. "Sorry, again. I am happy for Billy—it's wonderful that he'll get to go to college. And I'll definitely congratulate him later. But, right now, I just want to enjoy my dinner and talk to you. Okay?"

"All right, Steven," Melinda said with a sigh. "What's up?"

Steven didn't answer. He was so nervous that he didn't know what to do with himself. He'd gotten so tongue-tied when he'd seen her on the stairs that his daughter had been the one to tell Melinda how beautiful she'd looked. Plus, he'd picked the wrong restaurant, and he'd been rude to one of Melinda's mentees. Could things get any worse?

Thankfully, the server stopped by with their salads and a basket of warm rolls, and Steven managed to belabor the process of buttering his roll for another five minutes. When the silence began to grow awkward, he was saved again by the arrival of their salads, followed ten minutes later by their entrées. After saying grace, he sliced into his steak and stuffed a piece into his mouth, moaning softly as the exquisite flavors danced on his tongue. He looked over at Melinda and saw her close her eyes as she took a bite of halibut. How he'd missed watching her savor her meals.

When Melinda opened her eyes and saw Steven watching her, she raised her eyebrows. "What?"

"Nothing," he muttered. "I was just remembering how much we used to enjoy the food here."

The icy look on Melinda's face could have cooled off Texas in the midst of an August heat wave. She put her fork down and pushed her plate away. "Why did you bring me here, Steven?"

He was beginning to worry that the evening was completely falling apart. Why hadn't he realized that bringing Melinda to the place where he'd originally proposed to her with a plan of proposing again was a bad idea? He decided to be honest. "Look, Melinda. Maybe coming here wasn't such a good idea."

"Whatever," she grumbled. "Would you just tell me about the position so we can get out of here?"

"What position?"

Melinda rolled her eyes, then said, "Atlanta? Pastor Bernard's position?"

"Oh," Steven said, frowning. "That's right—Pastor Bernard called you this morning."

"Mmm-hmm. He said that he'd recommended me for the interim position." She pulled her plate closer to her and took another bite of her fish. When she'd swallowed, she said, "I'm very pleased and excited about this opportunity."

Steven felt like he'd lost control of the message he'd wanted to deliver. Shaking his head in confusion, he said, "What opportunity are you talking about, Melinda?"

"The opportunity to become the interim pastor of the Atlanta church, of course. What opportunity did you think I was talking about?"

Steven put his head in his hand. No wonder she hadn't refused to go to dinner with him. Bishop Johnson must have led her to believe that the dinner was to celebrate—or discuss—her finally getting her dream job.

He lifted his head and told her plainly, "I didn't invite you to dinner to talk about pastoring the Atlanta church. I wanted to ask you to marry me."

fourteen

MELINDA WAS GLAD SHE HADN'T BEEN CHEWING, for she surely would have choked. "Excuse me, did you just ask me to marry you?"

"Well, yeah, sort of. But I didn't mean for it to come out the way it did. I had this whole romantic evening prepared—the lights would be low, we'd be eating good food, and then, I was going to get down on one knee, just before dessert, and ask you to marry me."

"You brought me here to *propose*? Are you really that clueless, Steven?"

There was a tortured look on Steven's face that made her want to retract her words.

"When I made the reservation, it didn't seem like such a bad idea," he said. "Now, though, I see that this was the wrong place to bring you."

"How could bringing me to the last place where you proposed to me—and where you subsequently dumped me—be a good idea?"

"I know, I know. I'm sorry that I didn't think it through." Steven took Melinda's hand in his. "But I don't have much practice with asking women to marry me."

Melinda snatched her hand away. "If you ask me, you've had too much practice."

"I know that I hurt you when I let you go ten years ago. But, please, Melinda, don't punish Brianna for what I did."

Melinda was so angry that she didn't know what to say or do. Ten years ago, Steven had decided he no longer wanted her, but now that he needed a mother for his child, he had the nerve to come crawling back to her? "If you're looking for a mommy, Steven, why don't you stand outside one of the hundreds of day care facilities in Baltimore and find yourself one?"

"I'm not just looking for a mother, Melinda. I—"

"Take me home," Melinda interrupted him, pushing out her chair and standing up.

"Wait a minute, Melinda, please? Sit back down so I can talk to you. I promised you that I would be here for you forever, remember? Let me make good on my promise."

But Melinda wasn't interested in yesterday's promises. She'd spent a decade driving Steven's unmet promises out of her head, and she wasn't about to go back down that road again. "I'm leaving." She stalked away from the table and headed for the door, ignoring the maître d's astonished expression.

Steven jumped up from his seat and followed her out of the restaurant. "Don't leave like this, Melinda." He caught up with her, grabbed her arm, and gently turned her to face him. Then, he reached in his pocket and pulled out the ring box. "Look, I even picked out a ring for you."

When he opened the box, Melinda found herself staring at a three-carat, princess-cut diamond ring. It was nothing like the engagement ring Steven had given her when they'd been in their twenties—a skinny thing with a cluster of cubic zirconium. As beautiful as the ring was, though, Melinda didn't want it. Tears stung her eyes and began to stream down her face.

"Don't cry, honey," Steven said, reaching up to wipe her tears. "I know I did the wrong thing before, but I'm trying to make things right."

The door to McCormick & Schmick's opened, and the maître d' rushed out. "Are you all right, miss?" he asked Melinda.

"She's fine, thanks," Steven answered for her. "We were just having a discussion. Don't worry—I'll be back to pay the bill."

The man held up his hand. "I understand, sir, but I need to hear from the lady that she's all right. Do I need to call a police escort for you, miss?"

Steven flailed his arms as if surrendering. "Do you think I would hurt her? I just asked her to marry me, for goodness' sake."

Melinda didn't want to draw any more attention to their argument, so she spoke up. "I'm okay, sir—thank you for your concern. I assure you, I'm not in any danger."

"Are you sure?" the maître d' asked.

"Positive," Melinda said, putting a manufactured smile on her face.

"Okay, then," the maître d' said. Then, turning to Steven, he tacked on, "You be nice to the lady, y'hear? She's too beautiful to be crying."

"I promise," Steven said.

Melinda wanted to tell the maître d' that you couldn't trust Steven's promises…. When he'd gone back inside the restaurant, Steven turned to Melinda and said, "Wait here. I'm going to pay the bill, and then I'll take you home."

Melinda was tempted to call a cab, but she didn't want her dad or Brianna to wonder why she'd arrived home before Steven. So, while he paid the bill, she asked the parking valet to bring Steven's car around. She was waiting in the car when he came out of the restaurant and got behind the wheel.

They drove in silence for a few minutes. Finally, as Steven merged onto I-95, he said, "I don't understand why you're so upset. You and I belong together, Melinda. I'm finally facing that fact, but you're acting like I did something wrong."

Melinda fixed her gaze out the passenger side window, refusing to glance in Steven's direction. She didn't want to talk to him, either, but she had to know what he had decided to do about the interim pastor position at the Atlanta church. Still looking out the window, she asked, "Why didn't you offer me the pastoral position in Atlanta?"

"What?"

"You know I want to pastor a church, and Pastor Bernard specifically recommended me as his replacement." She turned to look at Steven. "Don't you want to respect his wishes? He probably knows what's best for his church—"

"I've asked Joel Lewis to be the interim pastor," Steven abruptly responded. Then, sighing, he added, "I honestly didn't think that the position would have been good for you."

Melinda scoffed. "Why? Because I'm a woman?"

"No...because I want my wife at home with me, not several hundred miles away."

"I'm *not* your wife," Melinda reminded Steven, "nor will I be." She turned back toward the window and watched the blur of buildings and landscapes until they reached her neighborhood.

When Steven pulled up outside her residence, Melinda jumped out of the car and ran to the front door. She unlocked the door, opened it quietly, and rushed up the stairs to her room before her father or Brianna could see her. Shutting her bedroom door, she collapsed on her bed in a state of confusion about the evening's events. When her father had called earlier, she'd thought that he and Steven had finally come to their senses and were going to offer her a pastoral position. But her father had been up to his old tricks of meddling in her business again...even though she'd asked him not to interfere.

A few minutes later, Melinda heard a knock at her door, followed by her father's voice asking, "Are you all right, baby girl?"

Melinda looked at the door and noticed that she hadn't locked it, but her father hadn't even tried the knob. That was unusual for him, and Melinda figured that he was feeling guilty about setting her up. Good. "I don't want to talk right now."

"Are you sure, honey? Steven and Brianna are gone. It's just me."

"I'm tired. I'll talk to you in the morning."

"Okay. But, if you decide you want to talk, I'll be up for a while."

Melinda didn't answer. She could tell that her father was still standing outside her door, but she just didn't have the strength to care. She felt numb as she lay down on her bed and pulled the covers over her without taking off her dress or shoes.

Once upon a time, Steven had meant so much to her. All she'd wanted to do was please him. But he'd asked too much of her—nothing less than the sacrifice of her dream—and had left her devastated when he'd refused to compromise. She still remembered that awful day when they'd sat in her father's office for their final premarital counseling session. It had been the day when everything had unraveled.

"Okay, since this is your final counseling session, I'd like to delve into some issues that we haven't covered yet," Bishop Johnson said to Melinda and Steven. "The two of you have been gushing over how much in love you are and how

you are so much alike. Now, I'd like you to do something that seems simple, but that a lot of people neglect to do before getting married."

"I've already picked up the marriage license, so, we're good, Bishop," Steven joked.

"That's good, son, but I need you to turn and face Melinda. And, Melinda, I need you to look directly at Steven, because I want both of you to tell the other what you want most out of life."

Melinda arched her eyebrows. "That's silly, Daddy. We both know what the other wants, because we want the same things."

"Okay, but do you know what you want from each other?" Bishop Johnson asked them.

"Of course, we do," Melinda said without a moment's hesitation.

Steven, however, remained silent. He took Melinda's hands in his and said, "Your father is right. We need to talk."

Melinda turned toward Steven with a look of concern. "What do you mean? What do we need to talk about?"

A pregnant pause filled the room as Steven hung his head for a moment. When he looked up again and opened his mouth, he began to speak the words that would break Melinda's heart. "I know you've been helping your father build the ministry at Omega."

"You've been helping, too," Melinda interjected.

"I know, baby." Patting her hand, he plowed on, "I just think you should know that I don't want my wife to work full-time."

"You've never said anything like this to me before," Melinda said.

"I know, but I've been thinking about this, and I want a wife who will stay at home with our children."

"I don't have a problem with stay-at-home moms—after all, my mother stayed home with me until she died. And, if I was planning to hold a corporate job or something like that, I would give it up in a minute in order to take care of our children. But God has called me to the ministry, Steven. Would you really want me to ignore the call of God on my life?"

Steven didn't answer.

Melinda turned to her father. "Dad, did you know Steven felt this way?"

"He mentioned it to me," Bishop Johnson said.

Melinda turned back to Steven and said, "I would never ask you to turn your back on God. How can you ask me to do such a thing?"

"I'm not asking you to turn your back on God. As my wife, you'll be the first lady of whatever church I pastor. Isn't that good enough for you?"

"No," Melinda said as she pulled her hands out of Steven's grip and stood up. *"I am a preacher, just like you. We shouldn't go into any church as pastor and first lady but as copastors."*

Steven shook his head. "That's not what I want, Melinda."

Melinda looked to her father for help. "Tell him, Daddy—God has called me to preach."

"I know that, Melinda," Bishop Johnson said, putting his hand on Steven's shoulder. *"But you need to understand what Steven wants and*

decide if you can live with that. Remember, a godly wife submits to her husband."

Seeing her father's hand on Steven's shoulder, Melinda felt as if this whole meeting had been nothing less than a conspiracy to get her to give up her God-given dreams. She folded her arms across her chest. "No, I can't live with that. But Steven has made me a promise—a pledge to marry me—and I've never had reason to doubt a word that's come out of his mouth."

The steady, unrelenting look on Steven's face prepared Melinda for what he would soon say....

Within a week of that counseling session, Steven had decided that he couldn't compromise. Looking back, Melinda was reminded that, as far as she was concerned, her father had conspired against her with Steven ten years ago, as well. She must have buried that memory. She was tired of the two of them trying to dictate the way she should live her life. She threw off the covers, sat up in bed, and picked up the telephone. Serenity had been after her for years to get out from under her father's thumb, but she'd kept telling Serenity that this was where God wanted her. She didn't feel that way anymore.

When Serenity answered her phone, the tears that Melinda had been holding back began to spill. This was too much for her to deal with. How could she go into work tomorrow and act like nothing had changed, when, in fact, everything had changed? The man who had broken her heart had thought they could just pick back up where they'd left off, as if his marriage to Sylvia had never even occurred.

"Tell me what's wrong, Melinda," Serenity urged.

"I—I need to come out for a visit. Are you too busy for company?" Melinda asked, wiping the tears from her cheeks.

"Why are you crying, honey?"

"I can't talk about it now, Serenity. I just need to get out of here."

"All right—I'll see you when you get here. And stop all that crying, girl!"

"I don't think I can," Melinda answered.

"It'll be okay. You'll see."

fifteen

STEVEN WAS DETERMINED NOT TO LET MELINDA GET away from him a second time. He had been committed to his marriage to Sylvia, but, to be honest, he'd always felt that their relationship had lacked something. Only recently had Steven realized that he'd never fallen out of love with Melinda, and it was sobering to acknowledge that he'd never truly belonged to Sylvia—that hadn't been fair to her.

He took a sip from his coffee mug and swallowed hard while thinking over his plan of action. Melinda had run inside without settling things the night before, and he'd let it go because he hadn't wanted to pressure her. But today was a different day. As soon as he got to church, Steven was going to go to Melinda's office and try speaking with her again. He didn't understand why preaching was such a priority to her. If she married him, she could be involved in *his* preaching—she could coach him, help develop his sermons. And she would still be involved in Missions and Community Outreach, or another ministry, if she so desired. Every preacher's wife he'd ever met headed up some aspect of the church, whether women's ministry or intercessory prayer or something else. Whatever she wanted—aside from preaching, of course—Melinda would be able to do as his wife. Why she couldn't see that, Steven just didn't understand.

He stood up and was rinsing his coffee mug in the sink when Brianna entered the kitchen, stuck out her arms, and twirled around. "I'm ready for school, Daddy," she announced.

Steven saw that her white, button-down shirt was spotless, her denim skirt wasn't wrinkled, and she was actually wearing the frilly socks he'd purchased for her a couple of weeks ago, which she'd said were too girlie. "You look sharp, sweetie," he said. "I like your outfit."

"Can we stop by Melinda's so I can see if she likes what I'm wearing, too?"

I guess my opinion doesn't count, Steven thought. "I'm not sure if Melinda wants to see us so early in the morning."

"She won't care. Ms. Melinda likes hanging out with me," Brianna told him confidently.

"I know she does. I'm just not sure that she wants to see me this morning."

Brianna put her hands on her hips and scowled at her father. "What did you do to her?"

Laughing, Steven held up his hands. "Nothing, I promise."

Brianna grabbed his hand and began pulling him toward the front door. "Then, let's go see her!"

Steven's plan had been to wait until Melinda had arrived at work and then approach her, but why not approach her at her home? And, with his cute kid at his side, how could Melinda refuse to see him? Maybe a good night's sleep had helped Melinda to accept the truth that they needed each other. Feeling a surge of renewed hope, Steven grabbed his keys and followed Brianna to the car.

When they arrived at Bishop Johnson's house, Steven felt a fluttering in his stomach that he hadn't felt since he'd been a teenage boy asking Melinda on their first date. As Brianna jumped out of the car and ran up to the front door, Steven gave himself a quick pep talk, grabbed ahold of his courage, and followed her up the walkway.

When Bishop Johnson opened the door, a worried frown passed over his face before he covered it with a smile. "Well, hello!" he said, ushering them into the house. "What brings you here this early in the morning?"

"I wanted to show Melinda my new outfit before going to school," Brianna said excitedly as she stepped into the foyer.

Bishop Johnson smiled and then sighed. "Melinda's not here, honey."

Steven looked at his watch. It was 7:45 a.m., and the church office didn't open until nine. "She left for work this early?"

"I don't think Melinda will be at work today." Bishop Johnson shook his head. "I should have known something like this would happen. She hasn't been happy since I decided to retire."

What Bishop Johnson didn't add was what Steven knew—that his decision to give Steven the pastoral position had compounded Melinda's unhappiness. Well aware of the part he'd probably played in her disappearance, Steven feigned ignorance. "What's going on with Melinda?"

"She moved out sometime last night...I found a note this morning."

Shocked, Steven managed to assure Bishop Johnson that he'd let him know the moment he'd heard anything from Melinda.

After dropping a dejected Brianna off at school, Steven drove to the church. He'd tried to call Melinda three times since Bishop Johnson had told him the news, but

Melinda hadn't answered her cell phone. When he arrived at the church, he stopped by Melinda's office, just in case she'd changed her mind about leaving town and was hard at work. Her door was closed, so he knocked twice, then opened the door. The room was full of furniture, office supplies, and personal belongings, but Melinda's absence made it feel completely empty. Steven closed the door and headed down the hall to his office. As usual, Barbara Peters stood up when he walked through the door to her office on the way to his.

"Good morning, Bishop," she said, handing him a cup of coffee. "I hope you had a nice evening."

Steven wished he could tell her the type of evening he'd had, but he wasn't interested in making another grown woman cry. "It was all right. Thank you for the coffee," he said as he took the cup and continued into his office, where he shut the door, sat down at his desk, and turned on his computer. Normally, he would work on his sermon for the upcoming Sunday for at least an hour before turning on his computer.

But, in his heart, he knew that Melinda wouldn't have just left without talking to him or at least sending him an e-mail message. He scrolled down the list of new e-mails he'd received. A lot of the senders were familiar to him— several pastors and committee heads—and many of the subject lines invited him to this or that event. But Steven wasn't interested in any of that at the moment. He was busily searching for an e-mail from Melinda.

Seeing no e-mails from Melinda, he decided to sign off and try concentrating on his sermon, hoping to stifle his disappointment. Before he could close his e-mail inbox, however, he heard the familiar *ding*, indicating he'd just received a new e-mail. He scrolled up, and there it was—a message from Melinda. His eagerness to hear from her suddenly vanished when he read the subject line: "Resignation Letter."

Why was she doing this? She didn't have to resign just because she didn't want to marry him. Wincing, Steven opened the e-mail and began to read:

Bishop Marks,

I would like to thank you for the opportunity that you and my father provided me to gain experience in ministry and missions by working at Omega Christian Church. However, it has become clear to me that I do not have a future at Omega or any of the other churches within our fellowship. Although it saddens me greatly to leave Omega, I must do so for my own peace of mind.

I wish you all the success in the world and ask that you accept my resignation. I wish that I could have given you the proper two weeks' notice, but, circumstances being what they are, I did not feel that I could continue to work another day at Omega.

Please give Brianna a hug for me, and tell her that I'll miss her more than words can say.

Sincerely,
Melinda Johnson

Steven closed his eyes, trying to imagine away the pain he was feeling. He'd done it again—he'd lost her. He lowered his head onto his desk and groaned. The way he felt was like watching Sylvia being pulled out of that car, limp and lifeless, all over again. Except that Melinda wasn't dead; she had chosen to remove herself from his presence. For the life of him, Steven couldn't get his heart to see the difference.

He finally lifted his head and began to compose an e-mail reply to Melinda. He wouldn't be proud of the way he was about to beg, but he was too desperate to care.

> Melinda, where are you? Please come home. I've been calling and calling, but you haven't answered your phone. I need to hear from you to know that you're okay. Will you please call me? I love you, Melinda. I don't know if I remembered to tell you that last night, but it's true. Please don't force me to live without you.
>
> Steven

His mind drifted back to the night he'd made a promise of forever love to Melinda. They had been young, in love, and living on the holiness of their parents. But, one night, they'd forgotten everything their parents had instilled in them about purity.

> Steven held Melinda in his arms as she sobbed. "I'm sorry, baby, I'm sorry," he said, not knowing what else to say.
> Melinda wiped the tears from her face as she told him, "We broke our covenant with God."
> When they'd been thirteen, he and Melinda had gone to Christian camp for the summer. The camp director had talked a lot about practicing sexual purity and waiting until marriage to have sex. At the end of camp, everyone had been invited to sign a covenant with God. Not all the campers had signed it, but Steven and Melinda

had felt that it would be the right thing to do, and they'd already decided not to have sex until marriage, anyway. After signing the covenant, each of them had been given a promise ring. So much for that promise, *Steven thought.*

"It will be okay, baby," he assured Melinda. "I promise you, I will make it right."

"It was just as much my fault as it was yours," she said, getting up and putting on her robe. She went into the bathroom, and Steven heard her blowing her nose. When she returned, he was fully dressed.

"I wanted to give you a present," he said, holding up a red rose from the bouquet he'd given her before dinner.

Melinda took the rose with a slight chuckle. "How many times do you think you can give me the same rose?"

"I wanted to give you a diamond ring, but I don't have the money right now." They were only eighteen, both headed off to college in the morning, with nothing but dreams between them.

"Steven, would you mind waiting downstairs while I get dressed? I don't want my father to come home and find you in my room."

"Sure, baby. I'll wait for you in the family room, because I want to talk to you about something." He turned and left Melinda in her room. While he waited in the family room, Steven paced the floor, trying to figure out the right way to ask Melinda to marry him.

"What are you doing?" Melinda asked when she caught him kneeling down in front of the lounge chair.

He stood up, trying to shake off his nervousness. "Practicing."

"Practicing what?"

"Sit down, Melinda. I want to talk to you," Steven said as he took her hand and then walked her over to the couch. When they sat down, he began, "I never wanted us to break our covenant with God. But, I can promise you this: it won't happen again until we are married."

With tears in her eyes, Melinda looked at him and asked, "You still want to marry me?"

"Of course, I do," he assured her.

She put her head on his shoulder and leaned against him. "I'm scared, Steven. I don't know if God will allow us to get married because of what we did."

If only he could rewind the years and keep his promise....

sixteen

I STILL CAN'T BELIEVE YOU FINALLY DID IT," SERENITY SAID, SIT-
ting with Melinda on the floor of her guest bedroom,
where used tissues had been strewn all around.

"I can't stay there. Not anymore," Melinda said, taking
another tissue from the box in front of her.

"Wow." Serenity leaned back against the bed. "I didn't
think you would ever leave your father's church."

"It's not my father's church anymore. The whole kit
and caboodle belongs to Steven Marks now."

"Yeah, but he asked you to marry him. So, it all would
have 'belonged' to you, too, just like your father wanted
to happen in the first place."

"It wouldn't be like my father wanted. Steven doesn't
want a copastor; he wants a first lady, and that just isn't
me." She wiped fresh tears from her eyes. "It doesn't matter now. I've decided not to work in ministry anymore."

Serenity sat up. "What are you talking about, Melinda?"

"I'm giving up, quitting, throwing in the towel…how-
ever you want to say it. My father and Steven don't think I
should preach, and I finally agree with them."

"But we've discussed this before, Melinda. Neither
you nor I can turn our backs on the call of God. Preaching is what we're meant to do."

As Serenity continued to talk about God's calling,
Melinda's memory drifted back nineteen years to the day

when she had broken her covenant with God. She'd always feared that she would pay a hefty price for what she'd done. "That's just it," she confessed to Serenity. "I do believe that God called me to preach, but Steven and I...." Her voice trailed off. She couldn't finish the sentence.

"What about you and Steven?"

Melinda thought she had cried a river already, but, somehow, new tears kept mingling with those that were drying on her face. She grabbed some more tissues and began to explain. "The day before Steven and I left for college, we sinned—we had sex. And, to tell you the truth, I've always believed that our sin was the reason our engagement ended the way it did."

Serenity scooted closer to Melinda and put her arm around her. "It's okay, Melinda. Mistakes happen."

"Let me finish," Melinda told Serenity, hugging her knees against her chest. "Steven and I made a covenant of purity with God when we were thirteen years old. Ever since I broke that covenant, I've wondered if God had decided He no longer wanted me to preach. Maybe that's why I've been struggling to preach and be heard all these years. And, maybe, it's just time for me to bow out and go get a job in the corporate world."

"'*All have sinned and fall short of the glory of God.*' Now, that's the Word, Melinda."

Melinda sniffled. "I know that. But, somehow, with all that has happened, it just seems as if God is trying to tell me to give it up. I failed Him long ago, and it's like He doesn't want to hear from me anymore."

"If that's true, then explain why Steven is still preaching. The two of you fell *together*. And the God I serve '*shows no partiality.*'"

"You're just full of Scriptures today."

"I'm full of Scriptures every day," Serenity said as she stood up and pulled Melinda up with her. "Come on. Let's go pig out on some ice cream sundaes. There's nothing like junk food when you're feeling down."

"Sounds good to me," Melinda said, following Serenity down to the kitchen.

The two friends sat at the kitchen table and gorged on ice cream sundaes with plenty of hot fudge sauce, whipped cream, and rainbow sprinkles.

When they'd licked their bowls, Melinda patted her full stomach. "If I keep eating like this, I'll be a couple sizes bigger by next week!"

Serenity waved off her worries. "A little indulgence every now and then never hurt anyone."

"Easy for you to say—you can still wear the size five jeans you wore in high school," Melinda told her as they headed back upstairs. Later, back in the guest room, Melinda tried to get some sleep. But her thoughts kept turning to the covenant with God she'd broken. She'd tried to forget about it, but Steven's coming back into her life had brought it all up again.

Melinda felt the urge to get on her knees and pray. So, she threw off the covers and got on the floor, bowed her head, and closed her eyes. "Lord, I truly love You," she began. "I have spent my life trying to bring others to the knowledge of You and Your saving grace, because I can think of no better way to live than to serve You. But I need to know what serving You really means for me. Am I called to preach? Or, do You have some other means of service for me that I've been ignoring in my determination to get into the pulpit?"

Tears sprang to her eyes as she thought about the guilt she'd carried, year after year, from one indiscretion.

The price of unending guilt was too high for one night of sin. If Melinda could turn back the clock and relive that fateful night, she wouldn't even entertain the thought of having sex with Steven. She lifted her face toward heaven and pleaded with God. "I believe that You are a forgiving God, but I have been held hostage by guilt for all these years. So, I'm asking You to help me to find the assurance of Your forgiveness. I want to be free from the guilt I've carried for so long. In Jesus' mighty name I pray, amen."

Melinda took her Bible from the nightstand and climbed back into bed. When she opened the Good Book, her eyes fell on the eighth chapter of John. She started reading with verse 36: *"Therefore if the Son makes you free, you shall be free indeed."*

Melinda smiled as that Scripture came alive to her. God was speaking to her, and she didn't want Him to stop. She flipped back to Psalms and came upon Psalm 103:12, which encouraged her further: *"As far as the east is from the west, so far has He removed our transgressions from us."*

"Okay," Melinda said, holding up her hands in surrender, "I get it. I've been forgiven, and I just need to accept it." She smiled as joy permeated her heart. She finally believed that her biggest mistake had not actually ruined her for the rest of her life, and that it had been her own guilt that had held her back. She refused to let guilt rule her life anymore. Maybe she wouldn't be in ministry, but God had good plans for her. Thanking God for His grace and mercy, Melinda lay down and went to sleep.

Although Melinda had gone to bed with God on her mind, she woke up thinking about Steven, partly because her cell phone's ring woke her up, and, when she went to answer it, she saw that the caller was Steven. He had called her several times the day before, but Melinda hadn't answered. She picked up the phone now and said, "Hello, Steven."

"Melinda! How are you doing?" Steven's voice was rushed, as if he was afraid she'd hang up before he could get a word in.

"I'm okay."

"Where are you?"

She was about to tell him that it wasn't his business where she was, but a quick reminder of God's forgiving grace tempered her response. "In Chicago. I'm staying with Serenity for a little while."

Silence filled the line. Then, Steven said, "Can I ask you something?"

"What?" She gripped the phone, trying to prepare herself for whatever he was about to ask.

"Do you love me?"

Startled, Melinda sat up and gripped the phone even more tightly. "Why would you ask me something like that?"

"You know why. I made a mistake when I left you ten years ago. But I never stopped loving you, Melinda. And, now, I need to know if you've stopped loving me."

"I can't discuss this with you right now, Steven. I'll talk to you later." She held her breath and pressed End before Steven could say another word. How could he ask her something like that?

After getting out of bed, Melinda showered and put on a pair of jeans and a pink T-shirt. She determined not to think about Steven for the rest of the day. She had more important things to worry about than her nonexistent love life—namely, discovering God's purpose for her life.

At breakfast, Serenity said, "Hey, since you're here goofing off while the rest of the world is working like Hebrew slaves, why don't you come down to the studio and help me with my show?"

Melinda spread a spoonful of grape jelly on a slice of toast and then looked up at Serenity with apprehensive eyes. "I told you last night that I wasn't interested in ministry anymore. Maybe I was being too hasty, but I'd like to spend some time seeking God's face and discovering just what He has for me to do."

"I'm not asking you to get out on the set and start preaching," Serenity said. "My assistant's on vacation this week, and I thought you might like to help me out. It would give you something to do...."

Melinda bit into her toast, mulling over Serenity's proposal. She swallowed, then asked, "What about my plans of seeking God's will? I can't exactly do that if I'm busy helping you all week."

"My assistant takes lots of breaks," Serenity assured her. "I'm sure you'll be able to find a quiet place to reflect and pray as often as you need to." Then, clasping her hands together, Serenity implored her, "Please? Come on, help a sister out."

Laughing, Melinda found that she couldn't refuse her best friend. "All right, I'll help you out this week. But I'm going to wear these jeans and this T-shirt, if that's okay." Melinda grabbed her purse and then turned back to Serenity. "Oh, and since I am unemployed, I will take room and board as payment for my services."

"That sounds fine. And don't worry about your outfit—you'll be behind the scenes, so it doesn't matter what you wear," Serenity said with a smile.

On their way to the studio, Melinda had been excited at the thought of having something to do besides sitting around Serenity's house and moping all week long. After no more than twenty minutes on the set, though, Melinda was convinced that Serenity had set her up. She hadn't watched the show for two nights, having been busy babysitting Brianna and making a mess of the dinner with Steven, and, so, as she was being briefed on her duties by the production manager, she found out that the title of today's show was "Women Struggling to Preach."

When she heard the topic, Melinda could only shake her head. Then, she took one of those breaks that Serenity had guaranteed her and set out to find a quiet, private place to pray. Before she ran out of the building screaming that she'd been set up, Melinda needed to know if Serenity had picked the topic on purpose, or whether it had been on the schedule in advance and Melinda's being there to hear it was a "God thing."

Finding a vacant lobby, Melinda sat down in an overstuffed chair, lifted her head heavenward, and prayed, "Lord, in my attempt to run from You, did I just walk into Your will for my life, anyway? Is there something You want me to receive from one of Serenity's guests today?"

Melinda sat there in silence, waiting for an answer from the Lord. She was determined to stay there until she'd heard from Him. All her life, she'd felt like she'd had to struggle to preach His gospel. Her father had been the only man in her corner, and even he had turned on her. So, now, her question for God was, if this thing was so hard, was she truly meant to do it?

"There you are," came Serenity's voice as she walked into the lobby. "I didn't think you would take your first break so early." With a smile on her face, she added, "I might have to dock your pay for this."

"You didn't tell me about today's topic of discussion," Melinda said with an accusatory tone.

Serenity placed her hands on her hips. "I guess that means you haven't been watching the show. We've been previewing today's topic for at least a week."

"I do watch your show almost every day," Melinda insisted. "I just had a lot going on this week."

"You'd better watch—I need the ratings," Serenity said with a laugh. She walked over to Melinda and pulled her out of the comfy chair. "Come on, I want you to meet someone."

They walked arm in arm back to the set where Serenity's program was filmed. It looked welcoming, with a bright-red chair and matching couch, both vibrant, like Serenity's personality. While her name conjured thoughts of someone calm and cool, who goes with the flow, those words didn't describe Serenity at all. She disrupted things, changed people's minds, and won them over to Christ's kingdom with gospel truth—and always in a bold, forthcoming way.

Melinda noticed a woman standing near the set with the sound technician, who was clipping a small microphone on her stylish, sand-colored jacket. When Serenity called out the woman's name, Melinda froze. She hadn't recognized the woman at first sight, but, now, getting a better look at her, Melinda could see that she was, indeed, Yvonne Milner, the famous copastor from Detroit, Michigan. Melinda had come to greatly admire this woman. She would even go so far as to say she was a fan of Yvonne's ministry. For the past two decades, she had dominated Christian television shows and conferences. If a ministry wanted to plan a successful conference, attempts were made to book Yvonne Milner. Women's conferences were not the only events at which she spoke, but they'd been where her ministry had been launched.

"Yvonne, I'd like you to meet my good friend, Melinda Johnson," Serenity said.

Yvonne turned to Melinda with a warm smile on her face. "So, you're the one Serenity tells me I have so much in common with," Yvonne said, giving Melinda a hug.

Melinda felt herself blush. "Well, I don't know about that, but I do love your ministry. I have about two dozen of your teaching CDs. You really bring the Word when you preach."

"Thanks, dear, though I can't take the credit. You know it's the Holy Spirit who speaks through me. And from what Serenity has told me, you bring the Word, too."

The associate producers were summoning Yvonne and Serenity, and, as they hurried over to the set, Melinda stood there, stock-still. She was so honored to have met Yvonne Milner that she could hardly formulate a coherent thought. The mere fact that such a powerful woman in ministry had heard about her and encouraged her brought tears to Melinda's eyes. Realizing that the filming was about to begin, Melinda took a seat in the audience. She hoped that Serenity wouldn't mind her watching the show instead of remaining backstage with the rest of the crew.

During the first part of the interview, Serenity discussed Yvonne's twenty years in ministry. She told the audience about Yvonne's soul-stirring messages, the tens of thousands of people who'd flocked to her various meetings, and the two dozen motivational books she had penned. Then, she turned to Yvonne and asked, "Tell me, how have you managed to do all these remarkable things in ministry when your husband didn't want you preaching in the first place?"

seventeen

WHEN STEVEN RECEIVED A PHONE CALL FROM THE nurse at Brianna's school, he got there as quickly as he could. He entered the nurse's office to find Brianna seated in a chair, holding an ice pack to her forehead. She looked up at him, and he saw eyes filled with sadness.

"I've got a headache, Daddy, and it won't go away."

Steven understood her pain. His heart was aching, too—and it had started when they'd found out that Melinda had left town without saying good-bye. Steven knelt down in front of Brianna and took her in his arms. His hug was meant to reassure her that things would somehow turn out okay. "I'm going to take you home, all right?"

Brianna nodded, then stood up and put her hand in her father's.

It was only noon when Steven took her home, three hours before school would let out, but he doubted she would have gotten anything out of her remaining classes. On the way home, he stopped at the local Cold Stone Creamery to buy Brianna an ice cream cone. It wasn't uncommon for him to stop there after taking Brianna to the doctor or dentist, because she always seemed to brighten up after watching the creation of her customized ice cream.

But, today, Brianna didn't even crack a smile when they pulled into the parking lot, and she didn't bother to list off graham cracker crumbs, strawberries, peanut butter cups, or other items to mix in to her usual double-scoop waffle cone. She simply asked for a single scoop of vanilla in a cup.

When they were back in the car, Brianna turned to Steven with anxious eyes and asked, "Did you call Ms. Melinda?"

"Yes, I did, Brianna."

"Did she tell you when she would come back home?"

Steven tousled his daughter's hair with one hand. This was just as hard for Brianna as it was for him. They had lost another woman in their lives. But he couldn't blame this one on a methamphetamine addict. He was solely responsible for Melinda running out of their lives like a wild mare from a rancher. "No, sweetheart, she didn't say."

"Do you think I did something wrong, and that's why she left?"

"Of course not, Brianna. Why would you even think something like that?" Steven asked.

"She left right after I spent the night with her, so I thought maybe I did something wrong," Brianna said, sniffling.

"Well, you can put that thought out of your mind, because Ms. Melinda enjoyed every minute she spent with you. She's missing you to pieces, but she just can't come back right now. That's all, Brianna. None of this has anything to do with you."

"Okay," Brianna said, but she didn't sound convinced.

At home, Steven grabbed his Bible and a notepad and took them into his office. He and his daughter might be sick at heart, but he still had a sermon to deliver on Sunday, and he wouldn't let his congregation down, no matter how much he wanted to throw on a pair of pajamas and stay in the house for the rest of the week.

Brianna sauntered into his office and asked, "Can I hang out in here with you?"

"You look sleepy, honey. Are you sure you don't want to go lie down in your bed?"

Shaking her head, she told him, "I want to stay with you."

When Sylvia had died, Brianna had become his shadow. He had allowed it because she'd been only five and had just lost her mother. But she'd come a long way toward independence since then, and Steven didn't want her to regress. Standing up, he prayed silently that God would give him the right words to say. Taking up his Bible and notepad, he said, "Why don't we go into the family room? We can talk a little bit, and then you can take a nap."

"Okay, Daddy." Brianna grabbed Steven's hand and led him to the family room, where she walked over to the television and turned it on. "Can I watch TV?"

As usual, the TV was set to the Word channel, the Christian network that they watched regularly. Steven picked up the remote control and pressed the mute button. "Maybe in a little bit," he said. "Right now, I'd like to talk with you, and then you can take a nap, if you feel like it."

"What do you want to talk about?" Brianna asked, settling on the couch.

"I want to make sure you understand that I'm not going anywhere."

"You can't say that, Daddy," Brianna pointed out. "You don't know what's going to happen tomorrow."

"I may not know the future, true, but I promise you that I'm—"

At the word *promise*, Brianna covered her ears with her hands. "No broken promises, no broken promises," she said, shaking her head.

Steven gently pulled Brianna's hands from her ears. "What's wrong, honey?"

"Don't make that promise, Daddy. Melinda's mom promised her that she wouldn't die, but she did anyway."

Steven pulled his daughter into his arms. He wanted to hug away the pain that she still felt over her mother's death, but he knew that he could never give enough hugs to take away that kind of pain, just as Bishop Johnson hadn't been able to hug Melinda's pain away. "I'm sorry, Brianna. I won't make you promises I can't keep, but I will try really hard to be here and to love you more and more every day that God allows me to live on this earth."

Brianna pulled away from her father's embrace as a smile crept across her face. "Okay, Daddy. I'll try to be here and to love you more and more each day, too."

"It's a deal. Now, lie down and take a nap so I can get some work done," he said, standing up so that she could stretch out on the couch. He spread a blanket over her, then sat down at the writing desk to work on his sermon.

The message Steven was planning for Sunday would deal with the subject of stewardship. His primary Scripture passage was Luke 16:1–12, and he opened his concordance to search for additional Scriptures to support his main points. He jotted down 1 Corinthians 4:1–2 and 1 Peter 4:10, then dived into the writing process. He would pray, think, and then write, or he would write, think, and then pray over something he'd just thought about.

After about fifteen minutes, Brianna stirred slightly. Steven looked over at her, and the TV screen caught his attention—Serenity's show was on. He'd watched her program on occasion, but didn't tune in regularly. Knowing that Melinda was visiting Serenity, though, he was interested in what she was discussing today.

Not wanting to disturb Brianna, he made sure the volume was turned down low before pressing the mute button on the remote control. Serenity had just welcomed her guest to the set, and he recognized her as Yvonne Milner. Steven had met Yvonne and her husband, David, while ministering at a men's revival at their church a few years ago. He'd found the husband and wife to be well suited for each other and very much in love. So, why was he caught off guard when he heard Serenity's first question: "Tell me, how have you managed to do all these remarkable things in ministry when your husband didn't want you preaching in the first place?"

Steven listened closely for Yvonne's response, not wanting to miss one word. "My husband wasn't just against me preaching; he was against all women preachers. As far as David was concerned, there was no such thing. And he frequently quoted 1 Timothy 2:11–14, telling me that I was supposed to be silent and not try to teach men in the church."

Steven was very familiar with that passage of Scripture. His father had opened his Bible to the book of 1 Timothy every time Melinda's desire to preach had come up. One day, when Steven and Melinda had been eleven, they had set up a makeshift pulpit in the Marks' backyard. His father had stood at the back door watching as he and Melinda had taken turns preaching to an audience of stuffed animals and action figures. When Melinda had gone home later that afternoon, his father had sat him down and told him that he was helping to send Melinda straight to hell for disobeying God. He'd read to him from 1 Timothy 2 and told him that God wanted women to be silent in church, that they weren't supposed to teach the menfolk anything.

His father had drummed those words into his head so often during his childhood and teenage years that, when Steven and Melinda had finally made plans to get married, he'd felt that he had to put his foot down and stop her from preaching.

Steven tried to drown out the words of his father as he turned his attention back to Yvonne. Serenity was asking her, "How did you cope with that for so many years without packing up and leaving?"

"Well, for one thing," Yvonne began, folding her hands in her lap, "I loved my husband, and I knew that God had sent him to me, so I would have been a fool to leave him." She looked out at the audience with a mischievous grin on her face and then said, "I'm not saying that Pastor Milner didn't spend quite a bit of time sleeping on the couch, though."

The camera panned the audience, and Steven saw many of the audience members laughing and clapping.

Yvonne continued, "But I soon found out that my fits and temper tantrums weren't going to change my husband's mind. So, I went to God about him. I prayed and I prayed. I spent so many years praying for God to change my husband's mind until, one year, I just gave up and started praying for God to change my mind."

The camera panned the audience again, and it was as if the cameraman knew exactly whom Steven wanted to see. The camera stopped and zoomed in on Melinda, who was sitting there, listening intently. Steven was struck by how beautiful she looked in a simple, pink T-shirt.

"That's Melinda," came Brianna's groggy voice.

Steven looked over at her. "I thought you were asleep!"

"I was, but I woke up. Why is Melinda on that show?"

Steven turned up the volume so they'd be better able to hear. "Serenity Williams, the host of the show, is her best friend. She's probably there to support her."

"Can you call in and tell Melinda that I miss her?"

"No, Brianna. It's not that type of show. I'll let you call Melinda tomorrow."

Brianna yawned. "Okay," she said, closing her eyes again.

Serenity's voice broke the silence as she addressed Yvonne again, saying, "But, evidently, God didn't change your mind, since you've been preaching and teaching the Word of God for almost twenty years now."

Yvonne smiled. "By the time I was ready to give up, God showed up and showed me and my husband who was boss. My husband can tell this story better than I can, because I was at home with a sick teenager when it happened. But, we had a visiting preacher from some small-town church that Sunday morning, and when the man had opened his Bible and preached from Joel 2:28–29, my husband told me that he'd begun to weep. When he came home that day, he was a changed man. He said that God had told him to stop stifling my anointing."

Steven turned the pages of his Bible to Joel 2:28–29 and read, *"And it shall come to pass afterward that I will pour out My Spirit on all flesh; your sons and your daughters shall prophesy, your old men shall dream dreams, your young men shall see visions. And also on My menservants and on My maidservants I will pour out My Spirit in those days."*

He closed the Bible as he remembered Melinda standing in the pulpit reading the passage from the book of Acts in which this prophecy is quoted. He turned off the television, got on his knees before the Lord, bowed his head, and simply prayed, "God, help me see it the way You see it."

Astonishment etched across Melinda's face as she listened to the wisdom that came out of Yvonne's mouth.

And, for the first time in a long while, she wondered if she could have made a happy marriage with Steven, even with his backward thinking concerning women in ministry.

When the interview was over and the show had wrapped, Serenity asked Yvonne if she would like to have lunch with her and Melinda. Melinda was thrilled when Yvonne accepted the invitation. She had so many questions she wanted to ask her.

At the restaurant, she played it cool for a while. Then, when their food had been placed in front of them and they'd said grace, she couldn't contain her curiosity any longer. "How do you know for sure that you should have married your husband? I mean, what if God wanted you in ministry decades ago? What if you could have brought hundreds more people to Christ, but those people are now lost because of your husband's stubbornness?"

Yvonne smiled and put her fork down. "Well, I guess I won't need this, because it will take me all of lunch to answer your mouthful of questions, my dear."

Melinda felt her face flush. "I'm not trying to stop you from eating. Please, eat. We can talk later," she said, feeling guilty for bombarding Yvonne with questions before she could get any food in her stomach.

"It's okay," Yvonne said. "I'm getting the feeling that this is personal for you, and that you really need me to answer your questions."

Melinda lowered her eyes and nodded as Serenity put in, "Melinda is going to be shy and bashful about this, so I'm just going to tell you exactly what happened." She gave Melinda an "I'm telling" look and then turned back to Yvonne. "Ten years ago, Melinda was engaged to a man who didn't want her to preach. They ended up calling off the wedding, but, now, he's the pastor of her church and the bishop of her fellowship. He still doesn't want her to preach, but he has asked her to marry him again."

"Oh, my goodness!" Yvonne exclaimed. "Are you saying that this man has waited ten years for you?"

"Hardly," Melinda scoffed. "He married someone else, but she died two years ago. And, now, he needs a mother for his seven-year-old daughter."

Yvonne put her hand over her mouth as her eyes flashed with recognition. When she removed her hand, she said in a low voice, "I think I know who you're talking about. Is it Steven Marks?"

Melinda raised her hands. "I don't want to name names." She then turned to glare at Serenity. "Especially since *somebody* just told all of my business."

Yvonne picked up her fork and knife and began slicing her steak. "You don't have to tell me who it is. But, if it is Steven Marks, I want you to know that I think he would make a wonderful husband."

"How can you say that? The man doesn't believe that women should preach, and I—" Melinda stopped herself when she realized she'd basically confirmed his identity.

"But you want to preach?" Yvonne asked.

Melinda considered Yvonne's question as she spread sour cream and salsa on her chicken quesadilla. Yes, until recently, she had always wanted to preach. But, just as Yvonne had gotten tired of the fight and prayed that God would change her mind, so, too, had Melinda. "I've always thought I wanted to preach. But, recently, I've been thinking that it might not be worth the struggle."

Yvonne nodded knowingly. "I used to feel the same way, Melinda. I struggled with my husband for so long over this issue, and we had so many fights, that I finally got tired of fighting."

"That's what I mean. I guess I don't understand how you agreed to marry him in the first place, since you knew his position on women in ministry," Melinda said.

"It's simple," Yvonne replied. She looked from Melinda to Serenity and then back to Melinda. "I loved David, and I couldn't imagine life without him. So, what you need to do is ask yourself this question: In the future, will you be happy without the man you love? Or are you willing to trust God to give you both—your ministry and your man?"

eighteen

EFORE GOING TO BED, STEVEN DECIDED TO PER-
form a quick Internet search about positions
on women in the church. They'd debated about
the issue during his years in seminary, but he couldn't
remember all of the arguments and counterarguments in
detail. In the blank space on the search engine homepage,
he typed the question, "What does the Bible say about
women preachers?" A whole host of results came up—
more than seven hundred thousand, in fact.

Steven clicked on one of the links and started reading.
This particular Web site used 1 Timothy 2:11-14 as the ba-
sis for its stance that women shouldn't preach, just as his
father had. It went on to say that since the Bible used the
masculine pronouns exclusively to refer to elders, bishops, and deacons, it meant that women shouldn't hold
those positions, either.

Steven opened his Bible and turned to 1 Timothy 2:11-
14, which he'd memorized in childhood. This time, however, he noticed something that he'd never paid much attention to before. He read the twelfth verse of 1 Timothy 2:
*"And I do not permit a woman to teach or to have author-
ity over a man, but to be in silence."* It was poignantly
clear to Steven what that verse was missing: God. Verse 12
didn't say that God does not permit a woman to teach or
have authority over a man; rather, the apostle Paul was stating his own opinion, based on the way he ran his church.

Steven looked at the Web site again and found another flaw in the thinking expressed by its author. He downplayed the roles of women from the Old Testament who had been in leadership or ministry, such as Deborah, a judge whose ministry he dismissed on account of the fact that she was one female judge among thirteen male judges. His assertion seemed to be that her being the minority proved that she shouldn't have been involved in ministry.

That didn't make sense to him, and he was reminded that the books of Exodus and Micah talk about Miriam's ministry—in Micah 6:4, she was even mentioned along with Moses and Aaron as one who led the Israelites out of bondage in Egypt!

The author of this Web site also mentioned Priscilla and other women from the New Testament who had ministered in some form but quickly rejected their ministries as illegitimate, as well. Yet, in Romans 16:3, Paul called Priscilla and her husband, Aquila, *"my fellow workers in Christ Jesus"*!

Nowhere on this Web site, or on any other site Steven visited that opposed women preaching, did he find any mention of Acts 2:17–18 or Joel 2:28–29, two other key passages that seemed to prove the contrary. Steven had read enough. He turned off the computer and went to bed.

In the morning, Steven suddenly felt like driving to Clinton, Maryland, to see his parents. He went to wake Brianna up. "Hey, kiddo! How'd you like to go with me to visit Grandma and Grandpa today?"

"Really?" Brianna asked excitedly, as she rubbed her sleepy eyes. "Can I spend the night?"

"Let me call first to make sure they don't have anything to do this weekend."

"Are you kidding?" Brianna jumped out of bed, ran over to her dresser, and started pulling out clothes and throwing them on her bed. "I haven't seen them in weeks—of course, they'll want me to spend the night!"

Steven went back to his room, picked up the phone, and dialed his parents' number. His mother picked up on the first ring. "Hi, Mom! How is everything? I was just calling to see if you and Dad were going to be home this morning. Brianna and I would like to stop by."

"Well, it's about time! We haven't seen you two in a month."

It was true, and Steven felt guilty. One of the reasons he'd been excited about moving back to Baltimore was that he would be living only an hour away from his parents. Since he'd taken the job, though, Steven had been to Clinton just once. "I'm sorry about that, Mom. I'll do better. But, hey, listen. Brianna wants to know if she can spend the night."

"You just get my little princess out here. Of course, she can spend the night."

"Will do. We'll see you and Dad in a little while."

By the time Steven and Brianna arrived in Clinton, Vicky Marks had arranged platters of scrambled eggs, turkey bacon, French toast, home fries, and buttermilk biscuits on the dining room table. Joseph Marks came downstairs in the navy-blue bathrobe Brianna had given him for Christmas. "Hey, Dad," Steven said as his father entered the kitchen and picked up Brianna, who squealed with delight.

"Hey, yourself, Bishop. How are things going at Omega?"

"Pretty well, thanks. I've got a few issues, but I'm hoping to resolve them soon," Steven said.

"Now, Joseph, you can talk with Steven about that stuff later," Vicky said. "Let's all sit down and eat as a family right now."

They sat around the table and said grace before filling their plates. As they ate, Brianna had a smile on her face that Steven hadn't seen since Melinda had left town. As she reached for another biscuit, she said, "Thanks for breakfast, Grandma Vicky. We never have anything this good at home."

"Hey," Steven protested. "I know how to cook."

"I know you do, Daddy. But your food is not as good as Grandma Vicky's."

"I guess I can't argue with you there," Steven admitted.

As he put a second helping of home fries on his plate, Joseph said, "It's a woman's job to cook, anyway."

Pointing her spatula at Joseph, Vicky said, "Don't you start that stuff this morning, Joseph Marks, or I guarantee that you'll be fixing your next meal yourself."

Joseph lowered his head and began shoveling food in his mouth without saying another word, and Steven sent his mother a quizzical look. He'd heard his father talk about gender roles all his life, but he'd never seen his mother show disapproval of anything her husband said.

When they'd finished breakfast and Vicky had cleared the table, Joseph looked at Steven and said, "Well, son, I suppose it's time you tell me why you drove out here this morning."

Steven pulled out his pocket Bible, opening it to Acts 2:17–18. He read aloud those verses Melinda had recently proclaimed at church, then closed his Bible and looked up at his father. Joseph's shoulders were hunched, and he wasn't smiling.

"Since I was a kid," Steven said, "you told me that God said women shouldn't preach. But these verses tell me that God is not necessarily concerned about whether a preacher is male or female; He will pour out His Spirit on us all."

"Is this about Langston Johnson's daughter?" Joseph asked, furrowing his brow.

Vicky was in the kitchen washing dishes, but, when she heard Joseph bring up Melinda, she came back into the dining room and said to Brianna, who was still sitting at the table, "Brianna, dear, would you like to read a book with me?"

"Yes, ma'am," Brianna said, following her grandmother to the living room.

"Why does this have to be about Melinda?" Steven asked. "I'm just trying to clarify something with you."

"Oh, so you think I'm wrong, huh?"

Steven shook his head. "I'm not saying that you are wrong or right. But I do want to look at this issue with you again and hear your side of it."

"My side?" Joseph asked with a tone of incredulity. "This has never been about my opinion." He reached over, picked up Steven's Bible, and flipped to 1 Timothy 2, pointing at verses 11 through 14. "See here? God says that women should be silent, and that they shouldn't preach."

"That's not true, Dad."

"What? Are you blind? Read the Bible for yourself. You'll see."

Steven put his hand over his father's and said, "I'm not calling you a liar, Dad. I'm just trying to show you that it wasn't God who said that women shouldn't preach. The apostle Paul was giving *his* opinion of what he believed women should or shouldn't do in church." Steven picked up the Bible and read verses 11 through 14 aloud, then set the Bible back on the table.

After a long pause, his father said, "That's the same thing your mother said. But, the way I see it, if the apostle Paul said it, then God said it. I'm an old dog, son. It's hard to teach me new tricks."

"What if you're wrong, Dad?"

"Hey, your mom tells me I'm wrong about one thing or another every day. What's one more thing?"

Steven looked deep into his father's eyes and saw a man who hadn't considered the changing times and probably never would. Steven only hoped that he would grow old with an open mind rather than the closed one he'd had for so many years. He got up from the table, hugged his father, and then went to say good-bye to Brianna and his mother, who were just finishing a book.

Vicky suggested Brianna take another book to Grandpa, and, when she was settled on his lap, she walked Steven to his car. He started the engine, put the car in reverse, and lowered the window to wave good-bye, and that's when she said, "Don't make the same mistake twice, Steven. Love that girl, and forget about what anybody else says."

Steven put the car in park and called back, "Is it that obvious?"

"You've got that same lovesick look on your face that you had right before losing Melinda because of you and your father's foolishness."

"I asked her to marry me, Mom." Flatly, he added, "She turned me down."

Vicky Marks put her hands on her hips and raised her eyebrows. "Then stop whining about it and go ask her again. You and Melinda belong together—you always have and always will."

Steven wasn't going to argue with his mother on that one, so he waved, backed out of the driveway, and headed toward Baltimore. He knew that he had a lot to think about before asking Melinda to marry him again. Melinda felt that she had been called to preach, and he had denied her the fulfillment of that calling at every turn. Now, as he drove north on I-95, he wondered if his reasons for denying Melinda what she wanted had been wrong—and if they had cost him the love of his life.

Feeling a little at odds, Steven didn't want to go home, so he took the exit that led to Omega Christian Church. There was always something going on at the church to occupy one's time and mind. On Saturdays, the kitchen would be teeming with members involved in the ministry to local homeless people, preparing food that they would later distribute at homeless shelters and in areas with high concentrations of homeless people. The classrooms would be filled with children between ten and eighteen years of age, participating in a tutoring program that helped them to develop their math, science, and English skills, among others. In the music hall, the praise dance team would be practicing.

Steven figured that he could help with the tutoring program. The church's office manager, Darlene Scott, ran the tutorial program, and so Steven went down to the classroom wing and sought her out. He found her in the hallway outside the math classroom. "Good morning, Bishop!" she said with a look of surprise on her face. "What brings you down here today?"

"Well, I've been hearing good things about the tutoring program, and I wanted to see whether I could lend a hand," Steven said.

Darlene blushed. "I'm honored, sir."

"Now, Darlene, if you could just tell me what you want me to do, I'll get to work."

"Oh, Bishop, the children would be thrilled to work with you. Let me check and see which classrooms need the most tutors today."

Steven considered Darlene as she shuffled through papers on her clipboard. She appeared to be about the same age as Melinda and he, but she was petite and soft-spoken—the complete opposite of Melinda.

"Hmm," Darlene said, lowering her clipboard. "Our math room has the most students today. Do you know the new math method?"

Steven stared back at her blankly. "The new what?"

"I'll take that as a no," Darlene said with a chuckle. "Do you know a second language?"

"I speak a little Spanish, but not enough to teach it. Is any help needed in the history or English classrooms?"

"No, I'm afraid that we have more than enough tutors for those subjects today." Darlene paused for a moment, then added, "You can help me out in the kitchen, if you'd like—I was about to start preparing the children's lunches."

"All right—since I'm not smart enough to be a tutor, I guess I can help with the lunches," Steven said.

"Now, Bishop, I never questioned your intelligence. You just don't have expertise in the subject matters where it's needed. To tell you the truth, neither do I. That's why I'm leaving my tutors with the students while I go make lunches," Darlene confessed.

Steven and Darlene went into the kitchen and worked side by side with those involved in the homeless ministry. After assembling thirty turkey sandwiches, Steven and Darlene put each of them on a tray, along with a bag of chips, a piece of fruit, and a can of juice. By the time they'd finished, more than an hour later, Steven was ready to head home and perhaps work on his sermon for Sunday.

When he got home, the house felt empty to him. Now that he had asked Melinda to marry him a second time, Steven realized just how much he longed to share his life with someone again. He had half a mind to pick up the phone and call Melinda. But the other side of his brain thought better of it. Melinda needed time, and he would just have to give it to her. He turned on the television in the family room for some company and soon fell asleep on the couch.

The next time Steven opened his eyes, he was staring at the nightly news. He sat up and was rubbing the sleep from his eyes when the newscaster made an announcement that woke him up all the way.

"I'm standing in front of the abandoned building where William Woods Jr., better known as Billy, was found shot in the back and legs. He's been taken to Good Samaritan Hospital. Billy was a varsity basketball player during his sophomore and juniors years of high school, but was dismissed from the team his senior year for substance abuse. The high school senior had been accepted at the University of Maryland, where he was planning to play basketball in the fall."

Reeling from this information, Steven picked up the phone and dialed Melinda's number, silently praying that she would answer—he didn't want to have to leave a message relaying such horrific news. On the third ring, he heard Melinda say, "Hello?"

Steven hadn't realized that he'd been holding his breath until he released it. "Hi, Melinda. It's me, Steven. I'm afraid I have some bad news."

"Nothing's wrong with my dad, is it?"

"No, honey, it's not your dad. It's Billy Woods. He's been shot."

nineteen

WHEN MELINDA'S FLIGHT ARRIVED IN BALTIMORE at ten o'clock that night, Steven picked her up at the airport and drove her straight to the hospital. "How's he doing?" was the first thing Melinda asked Steven when she got in the car.

"He was still in surgery when I left the hospital to pick you up."

"Oh, Steven, how could this happen? He was going to start college in a few months."

"Don't say *was*, Melinda. Billy *is* going to start college. He just needs to recuperate, that's all."

"Did I say *was*?" Melinda asked with a horrified expression on her face, then burst into tears.

Steven exited the highway and pulled into the parking lot of a gas station. He turned off the ignition and leaned over to take Melinda in his arms. "Stop crying. Billy is going to make it through this. You've got to believe me, Melinda, because I'm telling you the truth."

"How d-do you know?" she said between sobs.

"I've been praying for him all evening, and I trust that God will bring him through."

When Steven released her, Melinda leaned back against her headrest and wiped the tears from her face. Steven reached over to open the glove compartment, pulled out some tissues, and handed them to Melinda.

"Thanks," Melinda said, then blew her nose. "I didn't mean to say *was*." She took a deep breath to calm herself down, then said, "I'm okay now. Let's just get to the hospital, so I can talk with Billy's mother."

"Are you sure you're okay?"

Melinda squeezed Steven's hand. "I'm okay. And, Steven? Thanks for praying for Billy."

Steven nodded. "Hopefully, he'll be out of surgery by the time we get there."

They drove the rest of the way to Good Samaritan Hospital in silence, both too busy talking to God to talk to each other. When they arrived at the hospital, Steven parked in the garage and then raced Melinda to the waiting room outside the emergency room, where they found Brenda Woods sitting by herself on a couch. Melinda ran over to the woman and put her arms around her.

Brenda turned her face to Melinda's in a robotic fashion, and Melinda saw that her eyes were glazed over with grief. "You came?" she asked in apparent disbelief.

Melinda sat down on the couch next to Brenda. "Of course, I came. Where else would I be except here with you and Billy?"

Brenda put her arms around Melinda and held on for dear life, and Melinda's heart seemed to tear at the grief emanating from her. During her flight back to Baltimore, Melinda had been asking God how something like this could have happened. Billy had been changing his life around, moving in a better direction; now, he was lying on a table in the emergency room, having bullets pulled out of his body. "I'm so sorry this happened, Brenda. I just can't believe it."

Brenda released her and wiped her cheeks with the backs of her hands. Then, looking at Steven, who had sat down in a chair next to the couch, she said, "Thanks for comin' back."

"I told you I would," he said with an uncomfortable grin on his face.

"Billy will be so glad to know both of you were here," Brenda said.

"What do you mean, *were*?" Melinda asked. "I'm not leaving, Brenda. I'm staying here with you until we hear something about Billy."

"I'll be here, too," Steven said. "We wouldn't leave you alone at a time like this."

"I just don't understand why they did this to my baby," Brenda wailed.

"Do the police know what happened yet?" Steven asked.

Brenda wiped her freshly tear-streaked face on the sleeve of her sweater. "A witness said that Drake and Andre, they did this to my Billy. They're the ones who had him dealin' drugs, and they got mad when Billy stopped and set his sights on college. The witness said Billy was braggin' about goin' to college and playin' basketball, and so Drake got mad and started a fight with him." She shook her head and wiped away another tear. "I kept tellin' him not to hang around those boys. I knew from the moment I first saw them that they were goin' nowhere. In the past year, Drake and Andre have been at my house probably several times a week. They've eaten at my kitchen table. Billy thought they were his friends. But they shot him so he couldn't play basketball…? I just don't understand."

"That makes no sense to me, either," Steven said, looking just as shocked as he sounded.

"That's what the girl told the police. I hear Billy was winnin' the fight between him and Drake, and then

Andre said something about makin' sure that Billy never played ball again, and then he shot him. Then, Drake shot him, too."

"My Lord, my Lord," Melinda said, taking Brenda's hands in hers. "We need to pray."

But Brenda pulled her hands out of Melinda's. "I stopped going to church after my husband left me. I don't feel right turnin' to God for help after turnin' my back on Him."

"Brenda, whom did you think you were turning to when you asked me to take Billy to church all those months ago?"

"You," Brenda said with raised eyebrows, as if she didn't understand why the question was posed.

Melinda had quit her job at the church. She did not have a pulpit from which to preach, but she still worked for God. Everything that she did in ministry was for or because of the One who had saved her soul. "When you turned to me, Brenda, you were turning to God, because I am on this earth to live for Him—and to direct others to Him."

"And, besides," Steven chimed in, "God doesn't dole out blessings based on the things we've done right. If that were the case, a whole lot of prayers would go unanswered." Steven held out one hand to Melinda and the other to Brenda. "Will you pray with us, Brenda?"

Slowly, Brenda took Steven and Melinda's hands, and then the three of them bombarded heaven with their requests for Billy's complete recovery.

When the doctor came into the waiting room, his words would put their faith to the test. "Mrs. Woods?"

"That's me," Brenda said, standing up. Hesitantly, as if bracing herself for more bad news, she asked, "How is he doing, doctor?"

"We've removed the bullets. But I'm going to be honest with you, ma'am. We're going to have to wait and see whether or not Billy lives through the night. And, if he does live through the night, I can't promise that he'll walk again."

Brenda's hand went to her mouth as she doubled over and fell to the floor. Melinda wanted to scream at the doctor for his lack of compassion and tact. She wanted to tell him that they'd prayed for complete recovery, and that he needed to honor their faith.

Steven and the doctor helped Brenda up from the floor, and Steven took her back to her seat.

"When can we see Billy?" Melinda asked the doctor.

"He's going to be out for the rest of the night. If he wakes up, it won't be until sometime in the morning."

"Thank you," she said, then rejoined Brenda and Steven. It was at that point that Melinda realized no other family members were with Brenda. She would need someone at a time like this. "Do you want me to call anyone for you, Brenda?" she asked.

Brenda shook her head as new tears streamed down her face. "I've already called my family, but they all live in Florida. My husband's family hasn't had anything to do with us since he walked out." She hunched her shoulders. "It's just me and Billy. He's all I have."

Steven took Brenda's hand and squeezed it. "You've got us now."

A few moments later, a man ran into the waiting room. He was about as tall as Billy, with a thick mustache and sideburns. He rushed up to Brenda and asked, "What happened, baby? What's goin' on with my son?"

"William," Brenda said with a look of astonishment on her face. "How'd you know where we were?"

"I saw it on the news. Why didn't you call me?"

Her expression turned from astonishment to anger. "And listen to your girlfriend screen your calls so I can tell you your son has been shot? No, thank you."

Feeling like a third wheel, Melinda decided to get up and get a drink of water from a fountain in the hallway. Then, she sat down a few rows over to give Brenda and Billy's father some privacy. Steven must have felt awkward, too, because he immediately joined her after assuring Brenda that he and Melinda would be nearby if she needed them.

"Are you hungry?" Steven asked Melinda.

Melinda rubbed her stomach. "I hadn't thought about it before, but, yeah, I'm starving."

Steven looked at his watch. "The cafeteria is closed by now, I'm sure. Why don't I just order a pizza for all of us?"

"How long are you planning to stay, Steven? Don't you have to get home to Brianna?"

"Brianna is with my parents."

Melinda smiled. "I bet she's enjoying that. They've probably baked cookies, played a game, and watched a movie by now."

"They do spoil her," he said, using his BlackBerry to search for the numbers of local pizza places.

Melinda looked over at Brenda and saw that her estranged husband was holding her. She bowed her head slightly and thanked God for sending the one person who shared Brenda's pain equally and could provide some degree of comfort.

Melinda had been the person who'd most comforted her father after the death of her mother, and he'd been the greatest comfort to her, too. At some point in life, everyone needs a shoulder to lean on, and she had been proud to be that shoulder for her father. Watching Brenda lean on her husband's shoulder made Melinda feel ashamed of cutting her father out of her life without so much as a good-bye in person.

Turning to Steven, she said, "I'm going to make a quick phone call," then got up and walked down the hall to a bench between two artificial trees. She took her cell phone out of her purse and called her father. "Hi, Daddy! How have you been?" she said when he picked up the phone.

"Good to finally hear from you!" he said, and Melinda noticed that his voice sounded hoarse.

"You sound like you've got a cold. Is everything okay, Daddy?"

"I was asleep when you called. My voice is just a little scratchy."

"Are you sure?"

"Just a few aches and pains, that's all. Nothing for you to worry about. How have you been doing, baby girl? Are you still at Serenity's?"

She heard the things that her father hadn't said; she heard the sorrow in his voice and knew that he missed her dearly. Life was too short to let this issue keep them apart. Her father had lived for over eighty years; Billy, only eighteen, so far. But one thing she had learned tonight was that time spent with the ones you love is precious. A tear slid down her cheek as she said, "I'm sorry I left without talking to you, Dad. It just felt like you sold out on me again."

"I'm sorry, Melinda. I did ask Steven to give you the pastoral position in Atlanta, but he told me that he didn't want you to move to Atlanta. Steven is in love with you. He wants to marry you."

Melinda gripped her phone a little more tightly. She'd heard what her father had said about Steven, but, right now, she was concentrating on something else. "Did you ask Steven to give me that job because you felt guilty about giving him the position you'd promised me, or because you thought I was qualified for the position?"

"I don't just think you're qualified—I know that God has called you to preach. And I'm sorry if I gave you the impression that I no longer believed that."

"It's okay, Daddy. I forgive you." Then, wanting to check on Brenda, she said, "I'll be home in a little while, Daddy, but you'll probably be asleep. So, we can talk more in the morning, okay?"

"Where are you now?"

"At Good Samaritan Hospital. Billy Woods was shot earlier today."

"Oh, no, honey. I sure hate to hear that."

"Me, too. Please keep him in your prayers. I'll talk to you later, Daddy, okay? I love you."

"Love you, too, baby girl," she heard him say before she snapped her cell phone shut. She stood up and headed back to the waiting room, where she sat down next to Steven.

"I ordered an extra large pizza, half pepperoni, half deluxe," he said.

Melinda was amazed that he still remembered the way she liked her pizza. "Thanks," she said with a smile. "Any news while I was gone?"

"No, nothing. Any news on your end?"

"No, not really."

"Then, why were you crying?" Steven reached up and traced her cheek with two fingers.

Melinda quickly leaned away and brushed her face with her hand. "That was about another situation." She was going to elaborate, but Brenda suddenly shouted, "You're leaving?"

Melinda and Steven turned to look at Brenda. Her husband was standing and whispering something in her ear.

Brenda pushed him away. "Go. Get out of here, William Woods. We don't need you."

"Why are you so upset, Brenda?" he was saying. "I said I would be back in the morning. The boy won't even know that we were here tonight."

Brenda just stared off into space, not responding to the man in front of her. He finally turned and walked away.

Melinda grabbed her purse and went back to sit with Brenda. "Are you okay?" she asked.

"I'm used to it. I've never been able to count on William when it was necessary. He just never grew up, and I have to accept that."

"There is one good thing," Steven said, sitting down beside Brenda. "There'll be more pizza for us, since we won't have to share with him."

A smile crossed Brenda's lips, and Melinda was grateful to Steven for adding some humor to the situation.

"Speaking of pizza, I'm going to go to the main lobby to wait for the delivery guy. Can I get you each a soda?" Steven asked.

"I'll take a Mountain Dew or Coke," Brenda said.

Steven looked at Melinda and said, "Sunkist soda, right?"

"Thanks," she said, trying to hide her delight.

When Steven was gone, Brenda turned to Melinda and said, "Don't you let him get away. He seems like a real keeper."

Melinda looked at Brenda for a moment and then said, "I once thought so, too. We were actually engaged ten years ago. But he didn't want to be kept."

twenty

S THEY ATE THEIR PIZZA AND SIPPED THEIR SODAS, STE-ven and Melinda listened to Brenda talk about Billy's mischievous childhood and his lifelong love of basketball. Shortly after they'd finished, a nurse from the ICU brought over a few pillows and blankets. Before going to sleep, the three of them held hands and prayed that Billy would wake up soon and be able to not only walk, but also run up and down the basketball court.

Brenda slept on one of the couches in the waiting room; Melinda slept on the other. Steven took two chairs, put one of them against the wall and sat on it, and propped his feet up on the other. They'd decided that anyone who happened to wake up at some point throughout the night should go to the nurse's station and ask if there had been a change in Billy's condition. Twice during the night, all three of them were awake at the same time, and they prayed together for Billy before going back to sleep.

Around six in the morning, a nurse wearing a Sponge-Bob SquarePants smock came into the waiting room to inform them that Billy was awake.

Brenda stumbled to her feet. "Can I see him?"

"Of course, you can. Follow me," the nurse said.

Brenda turned to Melinda. "I'll be right back," she said, then followed the nurse down the hall.

Melinda rubbed her eyes and sat up, giving Steven a joy-filled smile. "He's alive, Steven. He's alive."

"Given how much we bombarded heaven with our prayers last night, I wouldn't be surprised if Billy was in his hospital room shooting hoops right now," Steven said. He stood up and stretched.

Laughing, Melinda said, "If he knows what's good for him, he'd better be resting."

Steven folded his blanket and set it on the chair he'd slept in. "I'd better head out—I've got to get ready for church."

"Thanks for staying at the hospital with us, Steven. I really appreciate what you did for Billy."

"I'll take you home, if you want, to shower and change your clothes."

Melinda shook her head. "Don't worry about me. I'm going to stay until Brenda comes back. Hopefully, I'll be able to see Billy, and then I'll have my dad pick me up."

Steven hesitated, then asked, "Are you sure? I mean, I can stay a little longer, if you want me to."

"You have a church service to get ready for. I am not going to hold you up any longer. Now, get out of here, okay?"

Smiling, Steven said, "Okay, but I'll be back this evening after I pick Brianna up from my parents'."

Melinda stood up. "I'll try to be here this evening when you come. I'd like to see Brianna."

"I hope you're here when I get back, too. I'd like to talk to you."

The look of longing on Steven's face made it evident to Melinda what Steven probably wanted to talk about. Her father's words from the night before were wreaking havoc in her heart. *"Steven is in love with you. He wants to marry you."* But Melinda was still trying to figure out who she was—and who God wanted her to be. There was no way she could be a wife right now. And, as far as

186 • Vanessa Miller

Melinda was concerned, Steven was ten years too late for marriage. But, if that was truly the case, why did she suddenly feel so empty now that Steven was gone?

Maybe Steven wasn't the reason she felt at odds with herself. Maybe it was that she missed Brianna. That little girl was so wonderful and so pitiful, all at the same time. Brianna wanted someone to replace her mother, but Melinda couldn't do that, no matter how much she loved Brianna. So, she prayed that the Lord would mend Brianna's heart. And, although it hurt her, Melinda prayed that God would send someone for Steven to love and marry. For Brianna's sake, as much as his, Steven needed a wife.

Melinda was pacing the floor of the waiting room when Brenda came back from seeing Billy, but her mind was so laden with thoughts of Steven and Brianna that she didn't know Brenda had returned until she felt a tap on her shoulder. Melinda jumped.

"Are you okay?" Brenda asked her.

"Yeah, I just didn't know that anyone else was in the room with me. How is Billy doing?"

"Okay. He was tired, so he went back to sleep," Brenda said. "Where did Bishop Marks go?"

"He had to get ready for church. So, I told him I'd get a ride from my dad."

"Nonsense," Brenda told her, waving her hand in the air as if shooing a fly away. "I'm going home to shower and change, so I can drop you off."

"I don't want to be a bother. You'll want to get back here as soon as possible—please don't worry about dropping me off."

"Billy's gonna be out for a few hours, so I have more than enough time to drop you off, go home and do what I need to do, and then get back here before he wakes up."

"Thanks, Brenda. I appreciate that."

"Not a problem." As they exited the hospital, Brenda added, "I wanted to ask you somethin' anyway." They got in Brenda's car, and, as Brenda pulled out of the parking lot, she said, "Before Billy went back to sleep, he told me to tell you that he'd crossed over. What did he mean by that?"

Melinda's face lit up. "Oh, thank God!" she said, and then asked, "Can I please see him when I come back this afternoon?"

"Sure thing. But please tell me what he meant by 'crossin' over.'"

Melinda smiled. "It's sort of an inside joke. The first time I met Billy, I was canvassing your neighborhood with some evangelists from my church. He saw us passing out tracts and told us to leave, because nobody there wanted to 'cross over'—to be converted to Christianity. So, every time I saw him, I would ask him if he had crossed over yet. He would laugh and tell me that he was young and had too much life left to live to serve Jesus. But I just kept praying for him anyway. And, now, I think Billy wanted us to know that if he had died yesterday, he would have been ready to meet Jesus."

"Are you tellin' me that my son's committed his life to God?" Brenda asked with a tone of disbelief.

"I can't be sure until I ask him, but that's what I think happened. Actually, I think he's probably wanted this all along, but he needed more time to warm up to the idea, to realize that serving God is the best way to spend his life."

Brenda was silent for the rest of the trip, save for the occasional "Okay" and "Uh-huh" in response to Melinda's verbal directions. Melinda figured Brenda was in deep thought; she just didn't know if she was thinking about Billy's recovery or his salvation journey. She gave Brenda the time she needed. When they pulled in front of her house, Melinda thanked Brenda for the ride and assured her that she would be back at the hospital in a little while.

After entering through the front door, Melinda walked down the hall and knocked on her father's bedroom door. "Is that you, baby girl?" her father asked from within.

"Yeah, Daddy, it's me. I just wanted you to know that I'm home."

"How's Billy?" he asked.

"He woke up, praise God."

The bedroom door swung open, and Bishop Johnson smiled at his daughter. He had on a pair of charcoal-colored dress pants, black socks, and a white undershirt. "That's good news, baby girl. I'm happy to hear it."

"You getting ready for church?"

"Yeah. Steven needs me to preach during the first service. He said he would get there in time to preach the second service."

"He was at the hospital with me all night, so I'm sure he needs to get a little sleep. Speaking of which," Melinda pointed to her room, "I'm going to take a nap myself. So, I'll talk to you later, okay?"

"All right, baby girl. You go get some rest. I'll talk to you this evening."

It was not until Melinda was in her bedroom looking for her favorite pair of pajamas that she remembered she had left her suitcase in Steven's car. She picked up the phone to call him, but then decided against bothering him. She'd already kept him out all night. She would let Steven get ready for church in peace.

After Melinda showered and got dressed for bed, as if it was eleven o'clock at night rather than eight o'clock in the morning, her father knocked softly on her door. "Melinda, honey? I just wanted to let you know that I'm leaving."

Pulling the covers over her, Melinda called back, "All right, Daddy. I'll talk to you later on."

She was asleep almost immediately, and, in her semi-comatose state, she drifted into dreamland. The next thing she knew, her father was standing at the front of the church with a Bible in his hands. But the pulpit was not in front of him. Had the praise dancers been performing, and had someone forgotten to put the pulpit back where it belonged afterward? Where were the deacons and the elders? Why wasn't anyone doing anything about the missing pulpit? Then, Melinda noticed that her father was standing under a wooden arch with lace wrapped around it. The arch also had pastel-colored flowers attached at the top and flowing down the two sides.

Music was playing, which served only to confuse Melinda more. Her father would never be standing in the middle of the pulpit area with a Bible in his hand while the choir was singing. But the choir was nowhere in sight. A woman stood off to the side, singing a song with words that Melinda couldn't quite make out.

The back doors in the sanctuary opened, and Brianna walked through them, wearing a pretty, cream-colored, floor-length dress. In her hair were the same pastel-colored flowers that adorned the arch, and she was carrying a basket of flower petals. When she started tossing the petals on the floor, Melinda finally realized that she was witnessing a wedding. She turned back toward the pulpit and saw Steven in a black tuxedo with a baby-blue vest.

Melinda's heart beat a bit faster at the sight of the man she had loved and lost. His eyes were so full of joy that it broke her heart to watch him standing there, getting ready to promise his heart to another woman. As everyone stood up, Melinda turned her attention to the sanctuary doors again. A woman in a strapless, ivory gown with a beaded, sweetheart neckline and a chapel train stood in the doorway. A twinge of jealousy crept up Melinda's spine, and she wanted to run to the back of the sanctuary and close the doors so that the woman couldn't walk through and steal the man who had belonged to her ever since they were children.

Why did she feel this way? She and Steven weren't right for each other—they never had been. They wanted different things out of life, out of marriage. So, why couldn't she accept the fact that God had finally brought a woman into Steven's life who would bring him joy? Melinda turned back to the bride, trying desperately to get a glimpse of the woman's face as she glided down the aisle toward the only man Melinda had ever loved.

"Who is she, Lord?" Melinda called out, unable to discern her face through the lacy veil.

The bride kept walking, the woman beside the piano kept singing, and Steven kept grinning. Then, all of a sudden, the bride dropped her bouquet, and the music stopped. She bent down to pick up her flowers, and that's when Melinda saw the woman's face as if she were looking in a mirror.

Gasping, Melinda jolted out of her dream and sat straight up in bed. She put her hand to her mouth as she tried to make sense of what she'd just seen. How could she have been that bride? And, if she had been that bride, why had she dropped the bouquet, and why had the music stopped? Melinda asked question after question that she had no answer to. She shook her head, trying to get the memories of that dream out of her mind. When that didn't work, she got out of bed, dressed, and grabbed her car keys.

It was 2 p.m., and Melinda decided to head back to the hospital to see if Billy was awake. She needed somebody to talk to, something to do, to distract her thoughts. When she got to the hospital, the nurse stationed at the door to the ICU told her that Billy's parents were in his room, so he couldn't have any other visitors right now. Melinda sat down in the waiting room and picked up a *Good Housekeeping* magazine to read while she waited. But she soon grew bored and hungry. So, she went down to the cafeteria and bought a turkey sandwich.

When Melinda returned to the waiting room, she found her father seated on one of the couches. She sat down next to him and gave him a kiss. "Hey! I didn't know you were planning to come here."

Bishop Johnson smiled. "I wanted to visit Billy, and I also figured this would be the only chance I'd have to talk to you today."

Melinda unwrapped her turkey sandwich and offered to share it with him.

"No, thanks. Barbara brought me some stuffed cabbage and meatloaf."

"That Barbara is always looking out for you. Why don't you just go on and marry her already?" Melinda asked jokingly. But, when her father didn't respond and she saw a guilty expression on his face, she quieted. "Daddy, can I ask you something?"

Bishop Johnson unbuttoned his coat and propped his feet on the coffee table in front of him. "What's up?"

"Why didn't you remarry after Mamma died?"

He quickly sat back up and cleared his throat. "Why do you ask?"

"I guess I just don't understand. I mean, I've seen how you act when you're around Barbara. It often seems that you love her, but you've never done anything about it."

He didn't deny Melinda's words but simply said, "It's complicated."

"How complicated can it be?" Melinda demanded. "Your spouse died twenty-eight years ago, and Barbara's died nineteen years ago."

"Yes, but I promised your mother that I would look after you. I couldn't very well do that while chasing after women, could I?"

"I'm a grown woman, Daddy," Melinda said, shaking her head. "Why don't the two of you just admit how you feel about each other?"

Lowering his head, Bishop Johnson told Melinda, "Barbara had been friends with your mother."

"What does that matter? Do you really think Mamma would disapprove? I'm sure she never expected you to spend the rest of your life alone."

Before Bishop Johnson could respond, Brenda and William Woods entered the waiting room. "I figured you were out here by now," Brenda said to Melinda.

Melinda noticed the tears in Brenda's eyes. "How's he doing?" she asked.

Brenda wiped her eyes. "He's awake, and he's asking for you," she said, sounding more upbeat.

Melinda stood up. "Can I see him now?"

William sat down and slumped in his seat. "I don't think that's a good idea," he said. His eyes seemed to hold more disappointment than he could bear.

"Sure, she can see Billy," Brenda said to her husband, then turned back to Melinda. "Before you go in, there's something you should know." Brenda hesitated, as if the message she had to deliver was too hard to say. She took a deep breath. "The doctor was right—he can't walk."

But we prayed about that, Melinda thought. Confidently, she said, "He *will* walk. God heard our prayers last night."

William jumped up and got in Melinda's face. "I don't want you goin' in there and fillin' my son's head with more Jesus stuff."

Bishop Johnson stood up and held out his hand. "Now, look here, sir. I need you to back away from my daughter."

Melinda put her hand on her father's shoulder. "I'm all right, Dad. Mr. Woods is hurting. I understand that." Then, she turned back to William and said, "I just want to see how he's doing and let him know that I'm praying for him—that's all. Okay?"

William relented and sat back down. "Just don't fill his mind with a bunch of useless hope."

He spoke like a man acquainted with useless hope and deflated dreams, and Melinda's heart went out to him. She herself had experienced some of the same when her own father had stepped in the way of her God-given dreams. "I wouldn't do that to Billy, Mr. Woods. You can trust me."

As a nurse unlocked the door to the ICU and led Melinda down the hall, she tried to prepare herself for the hopeless young man she was sure to see. Melinda couldn't imagine that Billy would be any other way after being in a room with William Woods Sr. for even a brief period of time. He had managed to pull her spirits down in the few minutes she'd spent with him in the waiting room.

But Billy was smiling when she walked into his room. "Hey, Lady J!"

"Hey, yourself, slugger."

Laughing, Billy said, "Now, it wasn't my fault. Those guys started that fight with me." He looked down at his legs and then added, "I guess they finished the fight, too. But, you know what? Those guys tried to take my life, but they really saved my life."

Melinda sat down in the chair next to Billy's bed. She didn't say anything at all; she was prepared to listen to Billy all night, if it would make him feel better.

"If they hadn't shot me, I don't think I would have crossed over. I kept thinking I was too young to serve the Lord—I had my life to live, with no time to give to Him."

"So, how does it feel?" Melinda asked.

"My dad doesn't want me to talk about it. He says that church and religion just give people false hope."

"Does your father have a problem with the church, or is it something else?"

"Well, he was drafted to the NBA after only two years in college, and he thought we were going to be set for life, but then he busted his knee. So, now, he's afraid of my getting my hopes up. But I don't think he knows what it feels like to be empty one moment and then have God's love flowing through your body the next. And that's how I feel...like this incredible love that I've never known has just become a part of my life."

"When did it happen, Billy? When did you cross over?" Using the phrase felt a little weird to Melinda, but, after she'd heard Billy describe his journey from feeling empty to being filled with God's love, she realized that it was a lot like crossing over from darkness into light—or love, as Billy explained it.

"I was lying on the ground where Drake and Andre left me for dead. Only thing was, I wasn't dead." He looked at Melinda and then asked, "Do you remember when you wanted to pray over my acceptance letter, and I said it was too late to pray, because I already had the letter?"

"Yeah, and I told you that it's never too late to pray."

Tears glistened in the corners of his eyes. Billy was looking heavenward as he said, "I remembered that when I was lying there, thinking I was about to die. I thought to myself, *Before I die, I'm going to pray.* But I didn't pray for God to save my life. I asked Him to take my life and use it the way He wanted to. I asked Him to forgive me for all the stuff I'd done wrong, and I know He did, because I feel different now."

"I'm so happy for you, Billy."

"I wish my father was. He thinks that I should be on a suicide watch or something since the doctors told us that I might not walk again."

"Your father did seem pretty upset by the news," Melinda acknowledged.

"I would be, too, if I believed it."

Melinda had promised Billy's father that she wouldn't get her son's hopes up, but she hadn't said that she wouldn't encourage Billy's own high hopes. "What do you believe, Billy?"

"I believe that God can do the impossible. I believe I will play ball again. And, when I do, I will let everyone know that it was God who healed me."

Melinda took Billy's hands in hers and said, "Let's pray about that."

twenty-one

BILLY'S WORDS OF HOPE HAD CAUGHT MELINDA OFF guard, but she hadn't let on while in the hospital room with him. Now, sitting in her enclosed patio with her feet propped up on one of the lounge chairs, she was alone with her thoughts. Melinda asked herself how she could have encouraged Billy to believe in the impossible when she'd given up on her dreams and quit the ministry because she no longer believed in the seemingly impossible. She had lost faith in the call of God on her life, and she had no one to blame but herself.

She had tried to lay the blame for her problems on Steven and her father, but it was she who had given up and decided not to preach. Instead of seeking out another church where female pastors were accepted, she'd simply decided that the fight was too hard, that perhaps she was never meant to preach, after all.

But, thanks to Billy, Melinda realized that nothing was too hard for her God. She no longer worked in ministry, she didn't have a pulpit from which to preach, but Melinda had faith that God would provide, according to His will.

No one could stop her from spreading the good news of Jesus Christ. She could go door to door, stand on a street corner and pass out tracts, help feed the homeless—there were limitless ways in which she could serve God, and she didn't need a pulpit to do them. Although Melinda admitted to herself that she still wanted the pulpit, she wasn't going to sit around pouting like a two-year-old until someone gave it to her. Starting tomorrow, she was going to take action. The first thing she needed to do was find a job, because her ministry would have to be funded, and she knew that the funds would need to come from her in the beginning.

A knock on the patio door drew Melinda's attention away from planning her destiny. When she looked up and saw Steven standing at the screen door, she smiled. He was no longer the enemy, but a friend who'd allowed her to lean on him when she'd needed him. "Hey, Steven. Come on out."

As soon as he opened the door, Brianna ran past him and almost knocked Melinda out of her seat as she hugged her. "You're home! You're home!" Brianna chanted happily.

"Well, of course I'm home, silly. Where else would I be?" Melinda asked, tickling Brianna.

Brianna laughed and tried to escape Melinda's grasp. "I didn't know if I would see you again. I thought I did something wrong, and that's why you left."

Melinda stopped tickling and gave her a concerned look. "Why ever would you think that?"

Steven finally came out to the patio, toting Melinda's suitcase. Brianna ran over to him and said, "Daddy, you were right. Ms. Melinda's not mad at me."

"I told you," he said. Then, he turned to Melinda and pointed at her suitcase, saying, "I thought you might need this."

"Thank you!" Melinda said as Brianna snuggled next to her on the loveseat. "I'd forgotten that you had it. I was going to wait at the hospital this afternoon until you got there, but I got tired and came home."

"There was a lot going on at church today, so it took a bit longer than usual to get out of there. And then, I still had to go to Clinton to pick up Ms. Brianna," Steven said, sitting down in the lounge chair next to the loveseat.

"Thanks for bringing it to me—I appreciate it. Did you make it out to the hospital after church?" Melinda asked.

"Yeah, we just left there. Billy was asleep, though, so we didn't get a chance to visit with him."

"Daddy talked to Billy's mom and dad about staying married," Brianna said.

Steven reached over and playfully pinched his daughter. "You weren't supposed to be listening."

"What did they say?" Melinda asked Steven. She wasn't sure he should have been counseling them—Brenda didn't deserve to take her husband back, only to have him keep cheating on her.

"They're going to get back together so they can help Billy," Steven told her.

"Well, Billy's not going to need them for very long," Melinda said.

Steven looked puzzled. "Brenda told me that Billy won't be able to walk. It seems to me like he'll need their help now—and for as long as they can offer it."

"For the moment, that may be true," Melinda conceded. "But Billy is a believer now. And he believes that God will allow him to walk again."

Smiling, Steven said, "I bet you had something to do with that."

"Yeah, I think I did. Billy showed me that the things we do in ministry matter, even when we don't think we're doing anything out of the ordinary."

Just then, the screen door opened, and Bishop Johnson poked his head out. "I've got *Dora the Explorer* on in the family room, if anybody is interested," he announced.

"My favorite show!" Brianna squealed, jumping out of her seat and running inside without another word.

Bishop Johnson looked at Melinda and winked. "I figured you and Steven needed a minute to talk."

"Thanks, Daddy—you were right. Enjoy the cartoon," Melinda said.

Bishop Johnson rolled his eyes, then closed the door.

Steven looked at Melinda with expectant eyes. "So, are we finally going to talk about my marriage proposal?"

"I guess I do owe you an explanation," Melinda said. She got up and stood at the back window of the patio, which overlooked the well-manicured backyard. Gazing outside, Melinda began, "I think I was about six or seven when I figured out what God wanted me to do with my life. From that day on, I only wanted to please Him. But, when you and I…slept together, even though we did it only once, it really hurt my Christian walk."

Steven got up and came to stand behind Melinda. "I'm sorry for the hurt I've caused you, but that was a long time ago, Melinda. Shouldn't we be able to move past that by now?"

"I thought I had," Melinda said, turning to face Steven with a sorrowful look. "Years ago, when my father told me that I would be the pastor of Omega when he retired, I felt like God had truly forgiven me for that night I spent with you. But when Dad changed his mind and gave the job to you, it was like God taking His forgiveness back from me. Like He'd never really forgiven me in the first place, and I'd been deceived all the times that I'd told myself I'd been forgiven."

"But that doesn't make sense, Melinda. I committed the same sin, so, if God forgave me, and I believe He did, why wouldn't He have forgiven you?"

"I didn't say that my thoughts made sense," Melinda said with the hint of a smile on her lips. "I'm just trying to explain my reaction to your marriage proposal."

"Oh! Well, then, let me sit down, because I want to hear this."

Melinda pointed a finger at him. "Don't start."

Steven held up his hands. "I'm not starting anything with you. I really want to hear what you've got to say."

"When you took me out to dinner," she continued, looking out the window again, "I thought you were going to offer me the pastoral position in Atlanta. So, when you proposed, instead, it was like hearing you say—once more—that a woman should stick to being the first lady of a church rather than being the pastor."

Steven jumped up again and put his hands on Melinda's shoulders, turning her to face him. "That's not what I meant at all. I didn't want to admit it, but I realize now that you would have been a great pastor for the Atlanta church. The truth is, I wanted you here with me. That was my underlying motivation. Don't you get it, Melinda? I'm in love with you. I always have been."

Melinda stepped back to put a little distance between her and Steven. "What about your wife, Steven? Did you love me while you were married to Sylvia?"

"I put you out of my mind while I was with Sylvia. And if she had lived, I never would have left her or moved our family to Baltimore with you here. But she's gone now, and I've come to realize that I need you in my life."

Melinda stood there staring at Steven, the man she'd loved so much when they'd been younger. She'd spent so many years trying to forget what that feeling was like that she honestly wasn't sure what she felt for Steven right now. And, she didn't know what to say to his declaration of love and need. She had trusted Steven with her heart once, and it hadn't turned out so well. Ever since, she'd lived by the adage, "Fool me once, shame on you; fool me twice, shame on me."

"You're not saying anything, Melinda. I want to marry you. Can't you give me an answer?"

"I don't know what to say, Steven. My life is a shambles right now, so I really don't know what I want to do about anything."

"What's wrong? If you talk to me, maybe I can help."

Melinda folded her arms across her chest and said, "For one thing, I don't have a job."

"You can have your job back at the church. Not a problem."

Melinda waved her hands. "I don't want that job back. I don't think it's a good idea for us to work together."

"Why not?" Steven asked.

"Because you don't believe in women preachers, and I still want to preach." She smiled confidently as she said those words. It felt good to know that she hadn't given up on God and His ability to make her what He wanted her to be.

"How do you know what I believe in?" Steven asked.

"Come on, Steven. I've known you since we were kids. I still remember the day you told me, 'My daddy says girls can't preach. Girls can only be mammas.'"

"Give me a break, Melinda. I was eleven years old."

"I don't want to hear it. You haven't changed a bit."

"Okay, fine. Come to church next Sunday and I'll prove that I've changed."

"What are you going to do, let a woman welcome the visitors?" she sassed.

"I guess you'll just have to come to find out, won't you?" Steven responded.

Melinda didn't answer. Instead, she walked over to her suitcase, opened it, and dug around until she found what she was looking for. "I picked up a gift for Brianna while I was in Chicago," she said, pulling out a plastic bag. She left Steven on the patio and went inside to the family room. *Dora the Explorer* was about to end, and her father was asleep in his easy chair.

"How was the show?" Melinda asked Brianna as she sat down beside her on the couch. "I bought you a little something while I was away...here," she added, handing the bag to Brianna.

"Really?" Brianna took the bag and opened it, then pulled out two DVDs—*Cinderella* and *Snow White and the Seven Dwarfs*. "You got these for me?" she said, giving Melinda a big hug. "Thanks!"

"I told you I was going to make sure you watched those *old* cartoons," Melinda said with a wink.

"Maybe Daddy will let me sleep over tonight, and we can watch them together!" Brianna said.

"You have school tomorrow, honey," Melinda reminded her.

Brianna looked up as her father entered the room. "Can I stay with Ms. Melinda tonight, and you can pick me up in the morning for school?"

"No, sweetie, you need to go home tonight," Steven said, then turned to Melinda. "What about Saturday? Brianna could spend the night with you, if you don't have plans already, and then you could bring her to church the next morning, since you'd be coming anyway—"

"I never agreed to attend Omega next Sunday," Melinda told Steven, raising her eyebrows at him.

"Please, please, say yes, Ms. Melinda. I really want to watch those movies with you," Brianna begged.

Melinda rolled her eyes and smiled. "How can I refuse when you ask like that? I'll pick you up on Saturday afternoon. So, make sure your bag is packed."

twenty-two

THE NEXT MORNING, MELINDA TOOK ADVANTAGE OF the fact that the church office was closed on Mondays and went to pack up her office in private. She would miss working with Darlene and Barbara—they had become constant sources of encouragement to her. She had even gotten used to seeing Steven in her father's old office and had grown comfortable working with him. But, if she wanted to pursue God's call on her life, she knew she had to go.

After she'd loaded her car with the boxes of her belongings, she went home and worked on her résumé. She spent most of Tuesday visiting Billy at the hospital. When a couple of Billy's friends from school came to visit, she went to the waiting room to sit with Brenda. "Is Mr. Woods coming to the hospital today?" Melinda asked.

"No. He's at work right now, and, when he gets off, a few of his friends will be helpin' him move his things back into our house," Brenda informed her.

Melinda pursed her lips and said nothing.

"You don't approve, do you?" Brenda asked.

Caught off guard by Brenda's question, Melinda said, "I guess it's not so much that I don't approve...I guess I just don't understand."

"What is it that you don't understand?"

Brenda's tone was calm, not indignant, and Melinda took a moment to consider what had been bothering her ever since Brianna had mentioned that Steven had talked to Billy's parents about giving it another try. "Well," she finally began, "he left you in the first place, right?"

"Yes, he did," Brenda confirmed.

"And, he's seeing another woman?"

Brenda sighed. "Yep, that's true."

"Then, how do you know he won't leave you again?"

Brenda leaned back in her chair with a thoughtful expression on her face, then turned to Melinda and said, "I don't."

Melinda stood up, walked a few paces, and then turned around to face Brenda. "I don't get it. How can you keep opening your heart to someone who might just turn around and leave you again?"

"Melinda, is this about me and William, or you and Steven?"

Melinda wanted to deny that she had even given Steven Marks a second thought. But she'd had that wedding dream again last night, and she'd awakened that morning with Steven on her mind. As she'd gotten dressed, she'd found herself wondering how Steven was doing at church. While driving to the hospital, she'd allowed her thoughts to turn to Steven again when a car had pulled up beside her at a stoplight and she'd caught a glimpse of the driver, looking Southern-preacher-fine in a suit similar to the one Steven had worn the first Sunday he'd preached at Omega.

Melinda sat back down next to Brenda. "Okay, I'll admit it—I can't get him off my mind. But he's the one who left me, and, now that he's back, I'm just supposed to fall all over myself to make him stay? I don't think so."

"But do you love him?" Brenda asked.

"I don't know," Melinda said. "I've tried to stifle my emotions where Steven was concerned for so many years that I don't know how I feel about him anymore."

"That might be your answer, then. Lord knows, William isn't perfect, but I've never stopped loving him. And that's why I'm willing to give this marriage another chance," Brenda said.

"I wish you and your husband all the best," Melinda assured her. "Please ignore my pessimism. I'm a work in progress."

"Not a problem," Brenda said. "I will tell you, though, I'm a bit surprised. I thought you Christians were big on forgiveness."

Melinda was ashamed of herself. She'd thought that God had placed her in the life of the Woods family to teach them about Him, but they had been the ones teaching her. Billy had helped her to believe in her calling again, and, now, Brenda had helped her to see the unforgiveness in her heart that she'd long overlooked. When Steven had left her and then married Sylvia two years later, Melinda had spent a lot of time in prayer trying to forgive him. All these years, Melinda had thought she'd forgiven Steven and moved on. But, maybe, she hadn't forgiven him at all, and it had simply been a case of out of sight, out of mind.

Melinda was beginning to realize that she had never resolved her feelings for Steven. If her feelings hadn't been all tangled up, would she have been able to say, "No, thanks," to his second marriage proposal and gotten on with her life? Why had she quit her job and left town? Was it that she'd been so full of unforgiveness for Steven that she'd had no room to explore any other feelings she might have had for him?

206 • Vanessa Miller

Lord, You helped me to forgive myself, she silently prayed. *Now, I need You to help me forgive others.*

She turned back to Brenda. "Thank you for your honesty, Brenda. After I visit with Billy, I'm going to go home and pray about this."

Just then, Billy's friends left, and Melinda and Brenda went back to Billy's room. After meeting Billy's friends and noting the well-mannered way in which they conducted themselves in public, Melinda asked Billy why he had decided to hang around guys like Drake and Andre when he had other friends who had obviously been raised right.

Billy hunched his shoulders. "Just being stupid, I guess. I started hanging around those guys when my dad left; I wanted to get back at him. When he didn't even seem to notice that I was doing drugs and had been kicked off the basketball team, I just kept hanging around with them and some other guys in our neighborhood."

"Well, as far as I can tell, he's noticing now," Melinda said.

"Yeah, but look what I had to go through to get him to see that what he did didn't just affect my mom—it affected me, too."

Melinda leaned over and hugged Billy. "Don't let what your dad did make you bitter. Just forgive him and move on. Love him for who he is." As Melinda said those words, she realized that she understood where Billy was coming from. After her mother had died, she'd shut out many friends and family members. And she was beginning to believe that her mother's death had a lot to do with the reason she was holding unforgiveness in her heart.

About half an hour later, Billy started complaining of pain. His nurse gave him some pain medication, and

Melinda and Brenda sat with him until he fell asleep. Then, Melinda drove home, went to her room, and got on her knees. She called out to God, begging Him to not just heal her heart but also show her what was in it. As God began opening her eyes and her heart, Melinda realized that she had been holding on to anger and unforgiveness since childhood. Tears streamed down her face as she prayed to God to take those feelings away. About an hour into her prayer, Melinda began moaning and groaning as the Lord conducted spiritual surgery on her heart. "Fix me, Jesus!" she cried out. "Fix me."

The process of being scrubbed spiritually clean was painful, but Melinda knew she would be the better for it once it was over. So, she stayed where she was and refused to get up until the job was done.

As she continued to cry out to God, her mother's voice began echoing in her head. *"I promise you, Melinda, I will always be with you."* Then, visions of her mother's final moments flashed through her mind. Usually, when Melinda thought about her mother, she remembered only two events: her mother making that promise, and her dying—breaking the promise.

Now, though, other memories flooded her mind— helping her mother set the dinner table, playing together at the park, laughing over inside jokes, and sharing long, warm hugs. It was as if God was showing her that her mother hadn't broken her promise at all. She was still there, locked away in Melinda's heart. Melinda's memories of her mother hadn't died, and, therefore, her mother would always be with her.

"I'm so sorry, Mamma," Melinda cried out. "I spent so much time trying to forget you because I thought you had broken your promise to me that I closed my heart to you."

Rejuvenated, renewed, and convinced that she had finally allowed God to cleanse her heart, Melinda pulled herself off the floor. As she sat down on her bed, she realized that her mother's death had affected her in ways she'd never truly understood. All her trust issues seemed to stem from that one broken promise, for, ever since her mother's death, Melinda had cringed whenever anyone had promised her something. The only people she'd thought she could trust to keep a promise had been Steven and her father, but, in the end, they had destroyed her trust, too.

She'd thought she had always trusted God, but she realized that her lack of trust in mankind had determined the way she'd treated Him, as well. She'd lived with an "I'll believe it when I see it" attitude—no promises necessary. And that was why she'd been willing to give up her dream of preaching. She hadn't seen any progress, and, so, her lack of trust had finally reared its ugly head in God's direction. But Melinda was a believer, and her desire to trust was stronger than her fear of broken promises, now that she truly believed God would never let her down. She determined to try giving others a chance to keep their promises—to be innocent until proven guilty.

What would it hurt if she took other people at their word? If someone failed to live up to a commitment, she wouldn't take that burden on herself. She wouldn't be responsible when others broke their promises. And she would live in God's forgiveness. These thoughts were freeing for Melinda, and, for the first time in hours, she smiled.

She was finally free, but she didn't want to be selfish about her newfound freedom. She got back on her knees and began praying for everyone she could think of. When she came to Brianna, it was as if the Lord was nudging her, causing her to look a little deeper. She asked God to reveal to her a way to reach Brianna and help meet her greatest needs, whatever they might be.

Soon, God began bringing to mind specific memories involving Brianna. Like the time Brianna had stood in her kitchen repeating, "My fault, my fault." And how she'd asked if Melinda had left town because she had done something wrong.

The Lord showed Melinda that Brianna was struggling to stay afloat in a pool of guilt that was about to drown her. She realized that, just as her mistrust of mankind had stemmed from her mother's apparent broken promise, Brianna's sense of self guilt came from blame she placed on herself for her mother's death. If Brianna didn't release herself from the guilt, she would grow up with just as many issues as Melinda had. Melinda couldn't let that happen. She wanted Brianna to have a happy, productive life, free of unnecessary guilt. Melinda opened her bedroom door with her mind set on seeing Brianna.

As she came down the stairs, she heard her father talking to someone in the kitchen. Curiosity got the better of her, and she peeked into the kitchen, where she saw Barbara Peters sitting across from her father at the table. Between them was a plate of chocolate chip cookies. As Melinda watched them converse, taking intermittent sips from their coffee mugs, she noticed that they weren't just talking; they seemed to be communicating something that only the two of them could comprehend. What struck Melinda was how comfortable they seemed together. They demonstrated the kind of ease and intimacy that comes only from a lifetime of friendship. The scene appeared as normal to Melinda as if her own mother were in the chair opposite her father.

Clearing her throat, Melinda entered the kitchen.

Barbara jumped. "There you are. I've been waiting on you to come out of your room."

Shaking her head, Melinda turned to her father. "Was I that loud?"

"I was worried about you," Bishop Johnson admitted.

Melinda had experienced only two other major meltdowns in her adult life—when her wedding was called off, and when Steven got married. Both times, her father had called Barbara to come over to the house to see her. He must have detected that this meltdown and prayer time had had something to do with Steven, or Barbara probably wouldn't have been there. Melinda gave her a hug. "You always come to my rescue, don't you?"

"You know I'm always here if you need me," Barbara told her.

Melinda sat down at the kitchen table with them. She looked from her father to Barbara and then said, "I'm okay. I truly believe that God has finally delivered me from many harmful things I've been holding on to."

Barbara's eyes lit up with joy. "Oh, sweetie, I'm so happy to hear that. I've been praying like crazy for you these past few weeks."

"Then, I guess it's my turn to start praying like crazy for you and my dad," Melinda said with a mischievous grin on her face.

"Do you know something we don't?" Bishop Johnson asked. "What's this crazy kind of praying that you're going to do for us all about?"

"I'm going to pray that God forces you two to set a wedding date and stop all the foolishness that has gone on for too many years. It's obvious you're in love. Just go buy the ring already," Melinda said and then grabbed a couple of cookies, stood up, and walked out of the house, shaking her head.

Melinda hoped that her father and Barbara would get their act together, but she couldn't sit at the house all night trying to point out the obvious. She needed to talk to Brianna. Before starting her car, she dialed Steven's cell number. When he picked up, she said, "Hey, Steven. It's me. Is it okay if I come over to see Brianna?"

"Of course—you're always welcome here."

"Thanks, Steven. I'll be there in a few minutes," Melinda said, then shut her phone to end the call.

She drove like a woman on a mission. And, since Steven lived only a few blocks away, it didn't take long for Melinda to reach his house. She jumped out of her car as if there was no time to waste. Billy Woods had almost gotten himself killed because of choices he'd made while trying to get back at his father. Melinda had spent a lifetime struggling to trust others due to a promise her mother hadn't been able to keep. Melinda was determined that Brianna would not go through life blaming herself for what had happened to her own mother. If Melinda had anything to say about it, Brianna would be free of guilt today.

twenty-three

STEVEN HAD NO IDEA WHY MELINDA WAS COMING TO visit Brianna, but he wasn't about to ask any questions. He just hoped that, by some small miracle, she would also decide to stay and talk with him. He ran around the house picking up socks, shoes, and anything else that looked out of place. In the kitchen, he put the dirty dishes that were in the sink into the dishwasher. She had already accused him of wanting a wife just so he could get a mother for Brianna; he didn't want her to think that he was looking for a housekeeper, too.

His love for Melinda was real. He'd denied it for ten years, but, now that he was back in the same town with her and seeing her as often as he was, he could deny it no more. Still, Steven was at a loss for how to convince Melinda that they belonged together. He had never been all that smooth when it came to women. When he'd dated Melinda, it had been easy; the two of them had grown up knowing they would be together. Sylvia had approached him and made the first moves in their relationship. So, Steven had never gotten much practice in pursuing women. Even though he knew Melinda better than any other woman, he still found it hard to come right out and say what was in his heart.

The house phone rang, startling Steven out of his musings. He closed his eyes and prayed that it wasn't Melinda calling to say she'd changed her mind. He picked up the receiver and said, "Hello?"

"Hello, Bishop Marks? It's Darlene Scott."

Steven smiled with relief. "Hey, Darlene. What's going on? You don't need my help making sandwiches today, do you?" he joked.

"No—today, I'm bringing the sandwiches to you. Well, not exactly sandwiches. But I cooked lunch for my book club and had some leftovers. So, I was calling to see if you and Brianna had eaten dinner yet."

"Thanks for thinking of us. I haven't fixed a thing."

The doorbell rang, and Steven's heart did a somersault. "Melinda's at the door. Do you have enough leftovers for her, too?"

"Sure do," Darlene said.

"Great—the two of you can stay and have dinner with me and Brianna. Thanks again, Darlene."

After hanging up the phone, Steven smiled to himself. God really knew how to bring a plan together. No way would Melinda refuse to stay for dinner when she knew that Darlene had gone to the trouble of making it.

⊙⫟⟋

After she rang the doorbell, Melinda waited for what seemed like minutes before Steven came to the door. "Sorry, I didn't mean to keep you waiting," he told her. "I was wrapping up a phone conversation when you rang the bell."

"Don't worry about it," Melinda said as she followed him into the house.

"You look like you've been crying," Steven said as he studied Melinda's face like a plastic surgeon preparing to perform a nose job.

Melinda was embarrassed that she hadn't remembered to wash her face after her exhilarating spiritual cleansing, so she tried to play it down. "I was in prayer for a while. No big deal."

"Looks like a big deal to me. Your eyes are bloodshot, and your face is streaked with dry tears."

"I got my breakthrough. That's why I'm here. God showed me that Brianna still needs her breakthrough. How about it, Steven? Are you ready to fight against the spirit of guilt that's plaguing Brianna?"

Steven stood still and stared at Melinda for a second. When he opened his mouth, he simply said, "She's up in her bedroom. Follow me."

Melinda trailed Steven up the stairs and down the hall, where he stopped at a door and knocked. "Brianna," he called, "you have a visitor. May we come in?"

When he opened the door, Brianna dropped two dolls and jumped up. "Ms. Melinda!" she squealed, running toward Melinda with open arms. The two hugged, and then Melinda sat down on the floor with Brianna. "Are we going to watch those movies you bought me?"

"Not tonight."

"Did you bring me another present?"

Laughing, Melinda said, "Not this time. I came over because I wanted to talk to you."

"Did I do something wrong?" Brianna asked, her voice quaking.

"No, sweetie, you didn't do anything." *Lord, please help Brianna*, came her silent prayer. *Remove the stain of guilt from her heart, mind, and spirit.*

"Are we still going to watch the movies on Saturday?"

Melinda smiled. "Of course, we are! I haven't forgotten. But I need to talk to you right now about something I was just praying about."

Noticing that Steven was still standing in the doorway, looking unsure as to what to do, Melinda motioned for him to sit down with them. Then, taking Brianna's hands, Melinda asked her, "Do you remember when I told you that the thing I remember most about my mother is a promise that she made and didn't keep?"

Brianna nodded.

"Well, because that was the thing I chose to remember, it haunted me all through my life. Because I felt like she had let me down, I stopped trusting other people—and had trouble forgiving them, too. I know firsthand how one destructive problem can grow into another, and I don't want you to live like that."

"I don't think I'm following you, Melinda," Steven said, looking confused.

"Don't you get it, Steven? Brianna's always asking if she's done something wrong or if this or that is her fault. All of this stems from her guilt over Sylvia's death."

Brianna looked stricken, then confessed, "I was talking to my mom when the man hit us. She always used to say that I talked so much that it distracted her."

"Wait, Brianna—did you hear what you just said? That *man* hit your car. He was responsible, not you," Melinda said, trying to reason with her. "Even if your mother hadn't been distracted, she wouldn't have been able to stop him from hitting your car."

"That's right," Steven chimed in. "The man who ran into you and your mom had taken something that had messed with his vision and with his ability to drive a car. The witnesses to the accident said that he was driving so fast, nobody saw him coming."

Lord, please increase Brianna's understanding, Melinda prayed. *Help her to understand what we are saying so that she won't go another day with this guilt on her shoulders.*

"Did you see the car before it hit you?" Melinda asked, trusting that God had directed her to ask that question.

"No. I didn't see it until it hit us."

"I bet Mommy didn't see that car, either," Steven said.

"She couldn't have, Brianna," Melinda affirmed. "Because, if she had seen it, she would have tried to avoid it in order to protect you. That car came from out of nowhere. And do you know whose fault it was?" Melinda asked, blinking back tears.

"Whose?" Brianna asked.

"That man who hit you. It was his fault, Brianna—not yours."

Brianna looked to her father, as if she was trying to understand some complicated equation, and asked, "It wasn't my fault?"

Steven pulled Brianna into his arms and held her close. "No, sweetie. It wasn't your fault."

Brianna turned around in his arms, looked over at Melinda and said, "It wasn't my fault." This time, those words were not in the form of a question. She spoke them with certainty, with the knowledge that she wasn't guilty.

Melinda moved closer and hugged Brianna from the front, so that her arms overlapped Steven's around the little girl. In that moment, feeling Steven's touch, Melinda realized that forgiving him had opened the floodgates for her to experience all the other emotions she had once associated with him. She lifted her head and looked into his eyes, and her heart overflowed with love and confusion at the same time.

Fortunately, the doorbell rang before Melinda could decide what to do with the emotions she was feeling. She didn't want Steven and Brianna to cut short their embrace, so she stood up and told them, "I'll get the door. You two stay here and talk."

Melinda felt as if she was gliding as she walked down the stairs. God had answered her prayers. Brianna was finally understanding that she'd had nothing to do with her mother's death. From this day forward, Brianna would be free of guilt—at least, where her mother was concerned. She'd probably find plenty of other things to feel guilty about as she grew into adolescence. Melinda prayed that God would help her to make peace with those things, as well, when the time came.

Melinda opened the front door. When she saw Darlene, she said, "Hey, girl! What brings you out tonight?"

Darlene held up a bag. "I brought dinner."

Melinda had been attending church long enough to be suspicious of single women bringing food to unwed pastors and bachelor bishops. Stepping aside so that Darlene could come in, she said, "So, um, how long have you been bringing food to Bishop Marks?"

"Well, let's see…I brought him dinner at church on Sunday, and I decided to bring him and Brianna the leftovers from my book club meeting this afternoon."

Melinda had seen this "The way to a man's heart is through his stomach" maneuver before, and she hadn't ended up on the winning side of that food fight. She wasn't about to go through that again. "Well, that's really sweet of you to make sure they're being fed."

As Melinda shut the door, Steven and Brianna appeared at the top of the stairs. Darlene held up the bag again. "Dinnertime!"

"Yes—I'm starving!" Brianna exclaimed as she bounded down the stairs in front of her father.

As far as Melinda was concerned, three was company, and four was a crowd. "I'll see you on Saturday, sweetie," she said to Brianna.

"You don't have to go," Steven said, following her to the front door. "Darlene brought enough for all of us."

If Melinda knew anything at all, she knew that Darlene did not want to feed her—not while she was trying to show off her culinary skills for the Bishop and his daughter. "Thanks, but I'm not hungry. I'll see you another time."

"Bye, Ms. Melinda," Brianna said, waving as Melinda opened the door, walked out, and shut it behind her.

She was heading down the walkway when she heard the front door open. She turned around to see Steven dashing toward her. "Melinda, wait!"

She stopped, but continued walking toward her car when he caught up with her. "Why are you leaving?" he asked. "I was hoping that we could talk tonight."

Melinda turned around at her car. "Talk to Darlene."

"Please don't do this, Melinda. I really wanted to spend some time with you."

"Really, Steven? This makes no sense. If you wanted to talk to me, why would you invite Darlene over for dinner?"

"I didn't invite her over. She called right before you got here. She had leftovers, so I told her to bring them on over. But I also asked if she had enough for you."

"How thoughtful of you," Melinda said snidely.

"What did I do wrong? I don't understand why you're so upset," Steven said with a look of puzzlement on his face.

"You didn't understand why it bothered me when Sylvia started bringing you pies on Sundays, either. You thought I was paranoid then, but you ended up married to her, didn't you?"

"Melinda, please stop being silly and stay for dinner. You helped Brianna get over the guilt of Sylvia's death. I owe you at least a meal for that."

"Sorry, Steven. I'm leaving. Please just go back inside and attend to your guest."

"Is there anything I could say to make you stay?"

"Nothing," she said, unlocking her car and getting in.

Before she shut her door, Steven asked, "Are you still coming to church on Sunday? We made plans, remember?"

"Yeah, I'll be there," she grumbled, then shut the door, started the car, and backed out of the driveway.

While driving home, Melinda told herself that she needed to find a new church. Because there was no way that she was going to continue attending Omega and watch Steven and Darlene fall in love.

Struggling to hold back tears, Melinda drove aimlessly through town. She didn't want to go home because Barbara might still be there trying to work things out with her father, and Melinda certainly didn't want to interrupt them. She didn't want to go to the hospital, either, because the last thing she wanted to do was upset Billy.

But, the fact of the matter was that Melinda was hurt, confused, and in love. She didn't know what to do or which way to turn. Part of her was glad that Darlene had showed up with her bag of "I'm the marrying type" food. If Steven chose to marry someone else, then Melinda wouldn't have to acknowledge her feelings. And she wouldn't end up marrying a man who would stifle her dreams. "Darlene can have him," Melinda said aloud as she continued driving.

But her words didn't actually match up with the feelings in her heart, because, as soon as she said them, a picture of Steven and Darlene appeared in her head, and the tears began to flow. She pulled her car into a strip mall parking lot, took out her cell phone, and called Serenity.

When Serenity picked up and heard Melinda crying, she said, "Oh, I'm so sorry, Melinda."

"M-me, too," Melinda blubbered.

"The last time I talked to you, it sounded like Billy was going to pull through."

Melinda pulled the phone away from her ear and stared at it. When she put it back to her ear, she said, "What? Oh, no, no—Billy's not dead."

"Then, why are you crying like this? Did something happen to your father?"

"N-no, Daddy is f-fine." Melinda rifled through her purse, looking for some tissues to wipe her face and blow her nose.

"Okay, now, I need you to stop crying and tell me what's wrong with you," Serenity demanded.

"I—I'm in love."

"Well, no duh. Why are you crying about that?"

Melinda finally pulled out a paper napkin from Wendy's and held it to her nose. "What do you mean, 'no duh'?"

"Girl, I knew you were in love with Steven when you quit your job and ran away from home."

"Shut up, Serenity. I'm a grown woman. I didn't run away from home; I left town."

"Whatever, girl. I'm just telling you that you aren't fooling anybody but yourself. So, you need to stop crying and go get your man back."

She had just told her father and Barbara something similar. Was she really acting like they'd been? Would she and Steven go around and around this issue for years with no conclusion? She really didn't want to handle her love life the way her father had handled his, but she appeared to be a chip off the old block in every way.

"Did you hear me, Melinda?"

"I heard you. I just don't know if I want a man who doesn't believe women should preach."

twenty-four

GET UP, BRIANNA, SWEETHEART. WE NEED TO GET TO church on time," Melinda said as she pulled the covers off of the sleeping child. Melinda's father had already left for church; he'd told her he was leaving early because he was picking up his date and taking her to breakfast, and Melinda had smiled. It was nice to finally hear her father admit that his outings with Barbara were actually dates. Hopefully, she would be attending a wedding soon.

Brianna stretched and yawned. "I'm tired. We stayed up too late."

"You're the one who wanted to keep watching all those movies, so, don't whine now. Just get yourself in that shower and put your pretty little dress on so we can go."

"Okay." Brianna crawled out of bed, took the washcloth and towel that Melinda held out to her, and went into the bathroom.

Melinda headed downstairs to make breakfast. When Brianna came downstairs, she asked, "You cooked?"

"Yep, I made us some pancakes. Let's chow down and then get out of here."

"Did you put cinnamon in the batter?"

"I sure did, so let me know if you like it," Melinda said, setting a plate of two pancakes in front of her.

Brianna sat down, poured syrup on her pancakes, and took a bite. "Mmm, you were right," she said. "Cinnamon does make things taste better."

After breakfast, they were about to go out the door when Melinda noticed a syrup stain on the front of Brianna's dress. "Oh, honey, you've gotten syrup on your dress—here, let me scrub that out." Melinda wet a dishcloth and dabbed at the spot. "At the rate we're going, we'll probably miss your daddy's sermon."

"Daddy's not preaching today," Brianna said, rubbing the front of her dress with a dry cloth Melinda handed to her.

"Who's preaching today if Steven isn't?" Melinda asked, grabbing her Bible, purse, and car keys.

"I don't know. He said something about a guest speaker."

Now, Melinda was curious. Why had Steven made a point of inviting her to church today if he wasn't going to preach? She could spend an entire day trying to get inside the mind of Steven Marks, but she didn't have the time.

When they arrived at church, Darlene was fulfilling her duties as a greeter. Brianna broke into a big smile and hugged her, and Melinda hated to admit her jealousy that another woman had elicited such a response. She held her breath, hoping that she wouldn't hear Brianna say that Darlene felt just like her mommy, too.

Seconds later, Darlene grabbed Melinda's arm and pulled her to the side. "Hey, Melinda—is everything okay between us?"

"Yeah, sure—why would you ask something like that?"

Darlene looked around, then said, "You didn't seem too happy about my bringing dinner for the Bishop and Brianna last week."

Melinda stopped trying to put up a front. "Okay, it did bother me a little bit, but then I realized that Steven can date whomever he wants. It's none of my business."

A dumbfounded expression crossed Darlene's face. "I'm not dating Bishop Marks—all the single women at this church know that's a lost cause."

Melinda wanted to ask Darlene what she meant by that. She almost took offense at the implication that none of the women at Omega wanted to date him. He was a good catch; what was wrong with them? But she decided that it wasn't her business. She gave Darlene a hug and said, "I'm sorry I was upset. I was just being silly."

After Melinda had reconciled with Darlene, she and Brianna entered the sanctuary and took their seats in the front pew. The worship music started, and Melinda sang praises to the Lord with the rest of the congregation. Brianna was rocking back and forth, engaged in worship as Melinda had never seen her before. It seemed that Brianna had a new lease on life, now that she was free from guilt, and Melinda was thankful for that.

When the music was tapering off, the doors on the right side of the sanctuary opened, and Steven walked in, followed by David and Yvonne Milner. Melinda was astonished. Yvonne looked down at Melinda and winked as she climbed the steps to the pulpit area.

Melinda smiled back at her. She was thrilled that Steven had invited David Milner to speak, and she hoped she'd get a chance to talk to Yvonne after the service. Yvonne would understand how she was feeling, and, maybe, she would be able to give her some more advice.

Steven stepped to the pulpit, looking handsome in a charcoal grey suit. He always took such care with his appearance, and it showed. As Steven addressed the congregation, he glanced in Melinda's direction and smiled. Her heart jumped, and then she rebuked herself. *Stop acting like a silly little girl. This man does not believe in your dreams. Don't let your heart's desires outweigh your mission in life.*

She turned her head, looked around the sanctuary, and nodded at a few people. Not wanting to appear disrespectful, she turned back around, but she didn't look directly at the pulpit. Then, she heard Steven say, "You all are in for a treat today. I've know the Milners for years, and they have always been gracious to me, even when I lacked understanding. So, I turned to them last week when I was desperately trying to figure some things out. After our conversation, I asked Pastor Yvonne to be our guest speaker today."

Melinda's head popped up, and she turned questioning eyes toward Steven. *Did I hear him right?* she thought. *Did he just say that he'd asked Yvonne to preach?*

"Many of you are familiar with Yvonne Milner's ministry, whether you've seen her on television or have read one or more of her books; I don't need to read her bio. As a matter of fact, I think she can speak for herself. So, I'm just going to hand her the mic and let her take it away."

Yvonne stood up, strode to the pulpit, and gave Steven a quick hug before taking over the microphone. "Thank you, Bishop Marks. I appreciate the invitation to speak at your church, and I believe that God has given me something to say. But, from what I hear, you already have a woman in this house with a powerful word for God's people." She looked at Melinda and mimed the tipping of a hat. "Keep doing what you've been called to do, Melinda. Because God is about to open a door for you that no man can shut. Do you hear me?"

The lump in Melinda's throat would not allow her to respond, so she simply nodded.

Yvonne opened the pulpit Bible and said to the congregation, "Turn with me to Genesis, chapter 37. I'm going to start reading at verse 5, so please follow along with me. *'Now Joseph had a dream, and he told it to his brothers; and they hated him even more. So he said to them, "Please hear this dream which I have dreamed: There we were, binding sheaves in the field. Then behold, my sheaf arose and also stood upright; and indeed your sheaves stood all around and bowed down to my sheaf." And his brothers said to him, "Shall you indeed reign over us? Or shall you indeed have dominion over us?" So they hated him even more for his dreams and for his words.'*

When she finished reading, she looked up at the congregation and said, "We've got some haters out there!"

Suddenly, the congregation was on its feet. The women stood up and cheered, as if they had been victimized and oppressed their entire lives by people who didn't want their dreams to come to pass. Melinda wondered if the men feared that Yvonne was going to raise a battle cry and tell all the women to stop cooking, cleaning, and showing love to their husbands until their demands were met, but Yvonne flipped the script.

She waited for the noise to die down and the congregants to take their seats before continuing, "But that doesn't mean we should hate back. Of course, other people are going to try to stop us from reaching our destinies. Of course, there will be roadblocks on the path to fulfilling our God-given dreams. But we can't allow ourselves to get bitter. No, we need to concentrate our efforts on becoming better.

"When I first told my husband I wanted to preach, he told me that I might as well forget about it, because no wife of his was going to be out preaching when she should be at home raising her children." She turned around to look at her husband, and when she faced the congregation again, her face showed the vestiges of a genuine, affectionate smile.

"Today, he's one of my biggest supporters. And do you know why? It's because I didn't become bitter. I allowed God to work things out between my husband and me."

Melinda thought about how bitter she'd become after her father had disappointed her. There was no denying it, so she wasn't about to try, but she thanked God that she hadn't stayed that way. She had learned how to call on God from an early age, so, when things had gotten so bad that she hadn't known what to do, Melinda had known she could cry out to Him and He would answer.

"I don't know what God has called you to do," Yvonne was saying. "But I know that He is well able to get you to do whatever He's called you to do. And I don't care what anybody else does—no one can stop a Holy Ghost plan in motion."

The congregation erupted with amens and hallelujahs.

Yvonne was on fire. She motivated the congregation like that for another twenty minutes. By the time she was finished, not only were men and women standing up and applauding her, but they were shouting how they would go after their dreams.

Yvonne raised her hand and then lowered it. "Y'all sit down. I promised that I would do something when I finished my sermon, and I can't give up this microphone until I do it." She turned and looked directly at Melinda. "I need you to come up to this pulpit area and have a seat."

Melinda smiled to conceal her confusion.

"You heard me right," Yvonne said, pointing to a vacant, high-backed chair behind her. It was an exact replica of the pastor's chair next to it, in which Steven was seated.

Obediently, Melinda got up and walked to the pulpit area. She paused in front of Steven, who said, "Sit down, Melinda. It's okay."

Then, Steven stood up and took the microphone from Yvonne. "What a word, what a word, what a word," he said as Yvonne sat down next to her husband. "Thank you, Pastor Yvonne, for gracing us with your presence today. I am humbled that you would choose to preach at Omega, knowing that you could have your choice of any pulpit in these United States."

Steven turned to the congregation. "When Pastor Yvonne said that we don't have to hate back just because someone else doesn't understand our dreams, that statement hit me hard. For a long time now, I haven't understood Melinda's dream of preaching. I thought that it was unbiblical for women to preach or pastor churches." He looked over at Yvonne and David as he said, "But some friends helped me see the truth, and I want to thank them."

Again, people began shouting amen and hallelujah as Steven walked over to Melinda, got down on bended knee, and said, "I know I've caused you more heartache than a woman should have to endure in one lifetime. I've been bullheaded and stubborn. But, today, I come before this congregation and announce that I believe you have been called to preach the gospel, and I will never stand in your way again."

Melinda was speechless. When Steven had asked her to come to church today, she hadn't expected to see a woman preaching in the pulpit. She hadn't expected to be seated in the pulpit area while Steven got on his knees in front of her, either. "What are you doing?" she whispered.

"Something I should have done a long time ago," he said, reaching into his jacket pocket and taking out the same ring box he'd showed her outside McCormick & Schmick's. When he opened it, the dazzling, princess-cut diamond glistened. "Marry me, Melinda, and share this pulpit with me. We belong together—in ministry and in life."

Melinda wanted to believe him, wanted to jump into his arms and accept the things he'd said. But they had fought for so long about their opinions on ministry that

228 • Vanessa Miller

she just had to ask, "When you say, 'share this pulpit,' what exactly do you mean?"

"I want you to pastor this church with me, Melinda, just as you should have done from the beginning. Say yes, baby. I promise I'll make you happy."

She heard his promise, and, for some reason, it didn't make her nervous. This wasn't like yesterday's promise. Instinctively, she knew that this was a promise for tomorrow, for the future. She wrapped her arms around him and freely kissed him.

The congregation stood up and erupted in cheers and applause.

Suddenly, Brianna joined them in the pulpit area, hugging Steven and Melinda. When they broke from the embrace, Brianna asked Melinda, "Does this mean we can bake cookies together whenever we want?"

With tears flowing down her face, Melinda said, "Yes, sweetheart. That's exactly what it means."

Discussion Questions

1. What do you think about women preaching? Did *Yesterday's Promise* help shape your view on this subject? If so, in what ways?

2. Why do you think that many people are against women becoming pastors? Are their reasons valid or not?

3. Melinda Johnson and Yvonne Milner both loved men who didn't believe in their calls to preach. However, the two women handled their situations differently. Who was right? Should a woman marry a man who doesn't believe in her call to preach? Why or why not?

4. In chapters 17 and 18, an argument is set forth concerning the right of women to preach the gospel. What do you think? Did Steven's scriptural research help you decide in favor of or against women preachers?

5. Hoping to get Melinda and Steven back together, Bishop Johnson took matters into his own hands instead of truly waiting on God. Do you see his actions as a lack of faith or just impatience?

6.   Melinda and Brianna both dealt with issues that stemmed from the deaths of their mothers. Can you think of an issue from a past incident that you haven't allowed God to cleanse and purge out of your life? How does the issue affect the way you live your life today?

7.   Melinda's struggle to preach became so hard that she began to doubt her calling. Has God ever asked you to do something that you thought was just too hard? Do you think He still wants you to do it? If so, what are you going to do about it?

About the Author

Vanessa Miller of Dayton, Ohio, is a best-selling author, playwright, and motivational speaker. Her stage productions include *Get You Some Business*, *Don't Turn Your Back on God*, and *Can't You Hear Them Crying*. Vanessa is currently in the process of writing stage productions from her novels in the Rain series.

Vanessa has been writing since she was a young child. When she wasn't writing poetry, short stories, stage plays, and novels, reading great books consumed her free time. However, it wasn't until she committed her life to the Lord in 1994 that she realized all gifts and anointing come from God. She then set out to write redemption stories that glorified God.

The Second Chance at Love series is Vanessa's first series to be published by Whitaker House. In addition, she has published two other series, Forsaken and Rain, as well as a stand-alone title, *Long Time Coming*. Her books have received positive reviews, won Best Christian Fiction Awards, and topped best-sellers lists, including *Essence*. Vanessa is the recipient of numerous awards, including the Best Christian Fiction Mahogany Award 2003 and the Red Rose Award for Excellence in Christian Fiction 2004, and she was nominated for the NAACP Image Award (Christian Fiction) 2004.

Vanessa is a dedicated Christian and devoted mother. She graduated from Capital University in Columbus, Ohio, with a degree in organizational communication. In 2007, Vanessa was ordained by her church as an exhorter. Vanessa believes this was the right position for her because God has called her to exhort readers and to help them rediscover their places with the Lord.

A preview of

Book Two in the Second Chance at Love Series
by Vanessa Miller

One

O ur wedding is next week, Michael. How can you
possibly have cold feet now?" Serenity asked
with her hands on her hips.

"This isn't about cold feet, Serenity. You're not listening to me. I've been trying to tell you for weeks that I
can't marry you."

This was not happening to her. This was some crazy
dream that she was going to wake up from any minute,
because there was no way that the good reverend, Dr. Michael Randolph—the man she loved and had been planning to marry for the past three years—could be standing
in front of her one week before the wedding, trying to
call it off. But, just in case this wasn't a dream, Serenity
decided to play along. "Okay, Michael. Please tell me exactly what I haven't been listening to."

Michael took off his black fedora, revealing his full
head of wavy, black hair, as he asked, "Can you sit down
on the couch with me so we can talk?"

She didn't want to sit down and talk; she wanted to
get married. Michael owed her a wedding. After all, she
had spent five years waiting on him. They had dated for
two years and then gotten engaged. That was three years
ago. She had told her friends that she and Michael had decided to wait until his ministry had gotten off the ground
before getting married, but in truth, it had been Michael's
decision to wait. Now that his ministry was growing, what

did he want her to do now—wait another five years so he could work on getting his church to a megachurch status?

Michael sat down on the couch and held out his hand to Serenity.

She sat down with him but said nothing.

"Serenity, the first thing you need to understand is that I love you more than life itself. It is because of how much I love you that I just can't go through with this marriage."

When am I going to wake up? Serenity held up her hand. "Wait a minute, now. I'm totally confused. Are you really telling me that you can't marry me because you love me too much?"

"Let me finish, honey," he said. He took a deep breath and then trod on. "It's this constant competition between us that's driving me crazy. I'm afraid that the love I have for you will fade because of the competitive spirit you have."

"The competitive spirit that *I* have!" Serenity exploded as she stood up. "I'm not in competition with anybody. I'm just doing what God has called me to do."

"That's what you tell people. But it's obvious that you are competitive. You wouldn't be where you are today if you weren't."

"Okay, what if I am a little competitive? What does that have to do with you and me? You're the pastor of a church. I don't have a church; I travel all over the world preaching, and I have a television ministry."

"See? That's what I mean," he said, pointing at her. Then, he stood up, too. "You're always throwing the fact that you have a TV ministry in my face. And you love it when other preachers invite you to speak at their churches. You've even been trying to get behind my pulpit for the past year."

"That is not true. I have never asked to preach at your church. I have more engagements than I can accept in a year, so I certainly don't need to beg someone for the opportunity to preach."

"See, there you go again. Every time you open your mouth, it's always something about what you're doing in ministry and how you're in such great demand."

It wasn't true. Serenity had never bragged about her ministry. At least, not in the way Michael was making it sound like she did. Yes, she was grateful that God had allowed her ministry to grow in the manner it had over the last two years. And, yes, she expressed that gratitude to anyone who would listen. But she wasn't bragging. She was trying to communicate to others that she understood how blessed she was. Serenity's father was the bishop of seven megachurches and ten small to medium-sized ones. He had often tried to get her to take over one of his churches, but she didn't believe that God was leading her in that direction.

She had stepped out in faith when she'd started her television ministry on a newly developed cable channel. Her television program was part Oprah, part Joyce Meyer in style. She interviewed many pastors and teachers of the gospel on her program. And then, when she was invited to minister, she brought along her camera crew and broadcast those events on her program, as well. She and Michael had discussed the format of her show at its inception. At the time, he had thought it was a great idea. He'd even told her that he could see her show going big time.

He just hadn't told her that, when it did, he would hold it against her. "Michael, please don't do this. Maybe we need to see a marriage counselor so we can talk this out before the wedding."

"Don't you find the fact that we would need a marriage counselor before we even get married a bit ludicrous?"

"Yes, but I also find your jealousy of a ministry that God's hand is on to be just as ludicrous." She took a deep breath, tried to calm herself, and said, "Look, Michael, I'm thirty-four years old. You're forty-two. We both agreed that now is the perfect time for us to have children. I waited for you for five years. Why are you backing out now?"

"I'm sorry, Serenity. I just can't marry someone who overshadows my own ministry. The next thing I know, people will be calling me 'Mr. Williams' instead of Randolph." He shook his head. "I just can't deal with that."

This was real. Michael was calling off their wedding, and Serenity felt as if her world was coming to an end. "What do you want me to do, Michael? Do you want me to give up my TV ministry? Is that it?"

He put his hat back on. "No. That won't work. You've created such a following now, that even if you weren't on TV, preachers would still be calling for you to preach at their conferences."

"I don't understand. I thought you loved me."

Michael didn't respond. He picked up his car keys and walked out of the house without looking back.

If he had turned around, he would have seen the tears that flowed down Serenity's face and the longing that she felt way down deep in her heart. But Michael didn't care about that. He cared only about being overshadowed. Why hadn't she seen this coming? Her best friend, Melinda Marks, had tried to warn her two years ago, when she'd said, "Trying to do the will of God and the will of your man gets hard sometimes." At the time, Serenity had thought that Melinda had been referring to her relationship with Bishop Steven Marks. Steven and Melinda had been engaged long ago, but Steven had felt that he couldn't marry a woman who wanted to preach the gospel rather than stay at home and be a wife and mother. So, he'd called off their wedding. But God's will had prevailed in that situation, and Steven and Melinda had finally gotten married eighteen months ago.

As she wiped the tears from her eyes, Serenity told herself not to worry. Michael would come to his senses, and they would be married on Saturday, as planned.

On Thursday, her father, Bishop Lawrence Williams, called and informed her that Michael's secretary was phoning everyone on the guest list and letting them know that the wedding had been cancelled. That's when Serenity finally faced the fact that Michael wasn't coming back. He had allowed his ego to override their love, and that was simply unacceptable to Serenity.

"Why didn't you tell me, sweetheart?" her father asked.

"I thought he would change his mind. I just didn't believe he was serious." Serenity had been calling Michael for the past three days, leaving messages on his answering machine and voice mail, letting him know that she still loved him, and that she still wanted to go through with the wedding. Why should she wait ten years for Michael to come to his senses, as Melinda had done with Steven? Serenity had been convinced that if they just went ahead and got married, they would be able to work everything out later.

"Why is he doing this?" her father asked, cutting in to her thoughts.

"He says I'm too competitive—that he can't marry a woman who overshadows him and his ministry."

"Oh, sweetheart, I'm so sorry to hear that. But if that's the way he feels, then he doesn't deserve you. I believe that God will send a preacher who can handle your anointing."

Serenity didn't say anything to her father, but as she hung up the phone, one thing was very clear to her. She wouldn't waist another minute of her life on another ego-driven preacher.